# The Phantom of Venice

Tired from her long, full day, Nancy quickly drifted off to sleep. But she was awakened sometime later by a piercing scream. She jerked upright, striving to clear away the mists of sleep from her brain.

A faint sheen of moonlight filtered into the room through the draperied windows—enough to reveal a dark something or someone in the center of the room.

Nancy's heart leapt. She reached out in the gloom for her bedside lamp and switched it on.

A hooded figure was moving toward Tara's bed! It seemed to hear Nancy's stifled gasp and whirled around sharply.

Her eyes widened in horror as she saw a hideous skull face!

# Nancy Drew
# Mystery Stories

## Available from MINSTREL Books

# 78

# NANCY DREW®

## THE PHANTOM OF VENICE

### CAROLYN KEENE

A MINSTREL® BOOK

PUBLISHED BY POCKET BOOKS

New York   London   Toronto   Sydney   Tokyo   Singapore

This book is a work of fiction. Names, characters, places and incidents are either the product of the author's imagination or are used fictitiously. Any resemblance to actual events or locales or persons, living or dead, is entirely coincidental.

 A Minstrel Book published by
POCKET BOOKS, a division of Simon & Schuster
1230 Avenue of the Americas, New York, NY 10020

Copyright © 1985 by Simon & Schuster
Produced by Mega-Books of New York, Inc.

ISBN: 0-671-73422-9

First Minstrel Books printing June 1988

10  9  8  7  6  5  4  3  2

NANCY DREW, NANCY DREW MYSTERY STORIES,
A MINSTREL BOOK and colophon are registered trademarks
of Simon & Schuster.

Cover art by Aleta Jenks

Printed in the U.S.A.

# Contents

# THE PHANTOM
# OF VENICE

# 1

## Mid-Air Meeting

The plane lights had been dimmed while the jetliner winged across the Atlantic through the midnight darkness. Nancy Drew had dozed off twice already during the flight from New York, but each time had awakened after only a short nap.

Why am I so restless tonight? she wondered. It can't be just the thought of riding in a gondola tomorrow and seeing the sights of Venice!

The famous young sleuth had been called to Italy to help solve a baffling crime connected with one of her father's law cases. The prospect was exciting, but Nancy had investigated many other mysteries before, and she was too experienced a traveler not to be able to sleep aboard a plane.

No, her restlessness tonight, Nancy sensed, had

1

nothing to do with crimes or mysteries, even in glamorous foreign settings. She suspected her unsettled state was an emotional response to a question that had been troubling her ever since her plane took off from Kennedy Airport:

*Am I or am I not in love with Ned Nickerson?*

Recently the two had decided to date other people and cool their own romance, which had been simmering since high school days. Since then, Nancy had had one or two romantic encounters which struck sparks, but Ned remained always in the back of her mind as someone safe and rocklike and comforting—someone she could always count on and turn to, no matter how the shifting winds of fancy might blow.

Their phone conversation just before she boarded the jetliner seemed to reignite all the feelings they had had for one another when they first met . . . and now, hours later, the warmth of that exchange still glowed in Nancy's heart.

Somehow, it seemed, she and Ned would always be on the same wavelength. But was that emotional rapport love?

She still wasn't sure . . .

With a sigh, Nancy flicked on her overhead seat light and glanced at her wristwatch. Almost 12:45. They had been in the air for six hours, with two more to go before landing in Rome.

Nancy set her watch ahead six hours to Italian time, then picked up the paperback mystery she'd been

2

reading, which had fallen into her lap the last time she dozed off.

A girl was walking up the aisle. Somewhat taller and slimmer than Nancy, she had straight, pale blond hair and large gray-green eyes, and looked about nineteen or twenty. Seeing a fellow traveler her own age awake, she smiled vaguely in passing.

Nancy returned the smile and was surprised when the girl stopped. "Mind if I join you?"

"Not at all. Please do!"

The other girl dropped into the empty aisle seat beside Nancy. There was something shyly appealing about her manner and appearance, Nancy thought.

"I expected the plane to be more crowded, didn't you?" she murmured.

"Yes, there must have been quite a few cancellations," said Nancy. "Not that I mind . . . I prefer having a little more elbow room."

"Have you done a lot of traveling?"

"Well, yes . . . a fair amount, I suppose."

"I wish I had! This is the first time I've ever been so far away from home on my own."

Nancy smiled again. "Are you on a vacation tour?" she asked politely.

"No . . . I wish I were."

There was such a sad, pathetic note in the girl's voice that Nancy immediately regretted having asked. "I—I'm sorry if I reminded you of something unpleasant," she murmured.

"You needn't be. I'd much rather be flying to Italy than staying in New York!"

Her response sounded defiant. Nancy was intrigued by her sudden change of tone.

"You live in New York City?" she asked.

"Yes . . . And you?"

"In a town you've probably never heard of, River Heights." As she spoke, Nancy found herself wondering about the other girl's background.

Her yellow silk shirt and beige designer slacks had obviously come from an expensive boutique, yet the total effect seemed oddly lacking in chic. It was as if the girl hadn't yet achieved her own distinctive style. The one uniquely personal touch was a flame-colored East Indian kerchief loosely knotted about her throat. It seemed to hint at secret fires within.

I'll bet she has plenty of spirit, deep down, Nancy speculated. She just hasn't learned how to express her real self yet.

As the thought flickered through her mind, she realized the other girl was studying her closely.

"Haven't I seen you somewhere before?"

Nancy shrugged. "It's possible."

The girl continued observing her for a moment, taking in Nancy's red-gold hair and vivid sapphire-blue eyes. Then she shifted her glance with a sudden awkward little laugh. "Sorry, I didn't mean to stare. It's just that your face seems awfully familiar. Maybe

4

that's why I sat down—because I thought we might know each other. My name's Tara Egan, by the way."

The teen from River Heights smiled. "Nice to know you, Tara. I'm Nancy Drew."

"*Nancy Drew?!* . . . Of course! I *knew* I recognized you. You're the famous detective who keeps solving all kinds of mysteries!"

Nancy nodded, slightly embarrassed. "I don't know about 'famous'. I've been lucky enough to unravel a few cases."

"I saw you on TV just the other day, in connection with some witchcraft case in England."

Nancy nodded again, racking her brain for some polite way to change the subject, as the other girl went on, "And now you're flying to Italy!"

"Yes, to meet my father. He's there on business. Er, whereabouts in Italy are you heading, Tara? Rome?"

"No, Venice."

Nancy smiled. "Well, well—small world! That's where I'm going, too."

"Hey, how about that!" Tara exclaimed. "I wonder if we'll be traveling together all the way?"

When they discovered that they were booked on the same connecting flight from Rome to Venice, she was delighted. "Oh, that's wonderful, Nancy! Suddenly I don't feel all alone any more."

"I'm glad, too, Tara. It'll be nice having company."

The discovery that they would be fellow passengers

all the way seemed to inspire Tara Egan to confide in her new friend. She explained that she lived in Manhattan with her mother and her mother's second husband, in a high-rise condominium overlooking the East River.

"My stepfather is a real estate broker," she added. Nancy was surprised at the sudden venom in her voice.

"You sound as though that's a crime," she said gently, smiling to soften her words. "I know several realtors back home who are very nice."

"You wouldn't think my stepfather's very nice," Tara retorted. "He's a slumlord."

"You mean he owns rental properties in poor neighborhoods?"

"Yes—and spends as little as he can to keep the places liveable. But mother thinks he's wonderful! They were both against my going to Italy. I was shocked, Nancy. I couldn't *believe* they'd try to stop me from going over to collect Daddy's last personal belongings. They said we could simply have them shipped to New York. Isn't that awful? Imagine not caring enough to go over to find out what happened to him, and how he spent his last days! I told them I was going anyhow—like it or not. I had enough money of my own saved up to pay for the trip, so they finally realized they couldn't stop me."

As Tara paused indignantly for breath, Nancy did

6

her best to sort out what she had been saying. "When did you last see your father?" she asked.

"About five years ago. He'd just come back to New York from the Far East and he called up—right out of the clear blue sky, you might say. Mom didn't want to see him, and she wasn't too crazy about me seeing him, either, but I made such a fuss that she finally had to agree. He took me out to lunch and dinner and a Broadway show, and then the next day we drove down to the Jersey shore and swam and laid around on the sand all afternoon, soaking up sunshine—it was just a terrific day! I loved every minute of it!"

Tara choked up for a moment, and Nancy saw tears glistening in her eyes. She squeezed the other girl's hand and said, "Your father spent most of his time out of the country, did he?"

"Oh, yes! Daddy traveled all over the world. In fact, from what Mom's told me about him, he always seemed more like an adventurer than an artist, which is what he was supposed to be. He could never bear to be tied down to one spot. That's what led to their divorce, I guess. He was the art director for an advertising agency when they were first married. But he quit to go paint in Mexico, and after that I guess he never did hold a steady job. He'd sell a few paintings through a gallery and use the money to go off and paint somewhere else. After a while Mom got tired of not having a home of her own."

"I can imagine," Nancy said sympathetically. "Did you hear from him after your parents broke up?"

"Oh, yes. He'd send me postcards and letters from all over, or copies of travel articles he'd written and illustrated for various magazines. . . . At least he *used* to. During the last few years, though, I didn't hear from him very often."

Daylight was already visible outside the window, and the plane's cabin lights had gone on. Nancy opened the curtains to the first rays of morning sunshine. She didn't mind the fact that she'd probably missed her last chance for a final nap before landing. She wasn't feeling at all sleepy, and she was too eager for another glimpse of Italy to want to drowse off again. Besides, people and their problems always interested Nancy, and she found Tara Egan's story genuinely engrossing.

"Had your father settled in Italy, or was he just visiting there?" she inquired.

"Oh, he'd been living in Venice for quite a while. He wrote me once that it was the most beautiful city in the world—the perfect place for an artist to live. He wanted me to come and stay with him, but he—well, he never had enough money to send me a plane ticket, I guess, and of course my mother and stepfather would never have *dreamed* of paying my fare just so I could see him!"

Again Tara's voice broke with an edge of bitterness, and again Nancy squeezed her hand.

8

"He must have been fairly young," the titian-haired teen murmured reflectively.

"Yes, he was in his early forties, just a year older than Mom. He died in an accident. He . . . he drowned in a canal."

"Oh, how awful, Tara! I'm so sorry. How on earth did it happen?"

"We don't know exactly. In fact we know nothing at all of the circumstances. We were simply notified by a telegram that gave no details—which is another reason why I made up my mind to go over."

The stewardesses began to serve breakfast, and the girls' conversation lagged. When they resumed chatting, Tara deluged the teenage sleuth with questions about her mystery cases.

Presently the pilot announced over the intercom that they would soon be landing, after which both girls become too excited and absorbed in preparing to disembark to have much time for talking.

At last the jetliner touched down, and the passengers filed out into a reception lounge at Rome's Leonardo da Vinci Airport. It was jammed with people waiting to greet arriving friends and relatives.

Lines moved quickly and within minutes after claiming their luggage, the girls cleared Customs. A single skycap in an orange uniform grabbed up both Nancy's and Tara's suitcases and led the way past busy airport shops and through a corridor that connected to the domestic flight terminal.

After less than half an hour's wait, they were able to board the airliner that would carry them to Venice. As they winged across the Italian boot, Tara fidgeted and chatted in bursts. She seemed to grow more and more ill at ease the closer she came to her destination. Finally she asked, "Will someone be meeting you when we land, Nancy?"

The strawberry blond shook her head. "No, Dad planned to, but at the last moment a business meeting was scheduled that he can't avoid."

"Then would you come with me?"

"Of course, if you'd like company."

"Oh, I would, Nancy! You see, Daddy wasn't living by himself in Venice at the time of his accident. He had a—an Italian lady friend." As she said this, Tara threw a sidelong glance at her companion. When Nancy nodded understandingly, she went on with a forced, nervous laugh. "Now that I'm almost there, I guess I'm a little uptight about meeting people and introducing myself as his daughter!"

Suddenly Nancy realized that her new friend was on the verge of tears again. She sensed, too, that for Tara, what lay ahead would be almost like attending her father's funeral.

"I'll be glad to come!" she said warmly. "And don't worry, Tara, you'll bear up, I'm sure of that. Just think how happy your dad would be to know you've come all this way for his sake!"

This time it was Tara who squeezed Nancy's hand.

10

As their plane circled in for a landing, the scene below was almost like a map. They saw part of the Eastern shore of the Italian boot, bordering the Adriatic Sea. The shoreline was indented by a vast shallow bay, or lagoon. This was protected from the sea by a thin sandy strip of shoal or beachland, called the Lido, which stretched across the mouth of the bay like a chain. Inside this chain, on the blue-green waters of the lagoon, floated the island city of Venice.

They debarked at Marco Polo Airport just outside the coastal town of Mestre. From here they rode a bus across the double railroad-and-car bridge, which extended out over the lagoon for five miles, to the nearest tip of Venice.

Thus it was from the bus window that the two girls had their first glimpse of the lovely city rising from the water, the *Serenissima,* or Most Serene, as Venice was called centuries ago, when she was an independent republic and a great maritime power.

"Isn't it beautiful!" said Tara. "Just like all the pictures I've ever seen of it. But I still don't understand why they built Venice on water."

"From what I've read," said Nancy, "they hadn't much choice. Rome was crumbling, and Italy was being invaded by barbarians. The only place people could take refuge was on the marshy little islands out in the lagoon. And their settlement gradually turned into Venice."

11

"When you think of it like that, the result seems almost like magic!"

The bus left them on the car-landing, called the *Piazzale Roma*, just across the Grand Canal from the Santa Lucia train station. The place was a beehive of activity. A *vaporetto*, one of the steam launches that serve as public buses in Venice, was unloading passengers, prior to leaving on a return trip down the canal.

Tara said that her travel agent, for reasons of economy, had booked her into a *pensione*, or boarding house, rather than a hotel. "It's in the San Polo district," she said, fishing out the address.

"Oh, good! We're in San Polo now," said Nancy. "That's the first district on the Right Bank of the Grand Canal. We might even be able to walk it from here, if we had no luggage to carry."

In the end, the girls hired a gondola, which soon deposited them on the narrow quay in front of a pink-stuccoed house with a sign over the door, *Pensione Dandolo*.

The motherly landlady, Signora Dandolo, welcomed her new guest with a warm smile and readily agreed that Nancy could leave her suitcases in Tara's room while the two girls went on to the home of Tara's late father.

"Ah, *si!* That is only a few minutes' walk from here!" Mrs. Dandolo told them after hearing the address. "My son, Zorzi, will show you the way!"

The lively ten-year-old proudly escorted the two

pretty *Americane* to their destination, a stately but rather narrow, yellowish-brown building that looked about two centuries old.

"*Grazie tanto, Signorine!*" the boy exclaimed when the girls tipped him. "Any time you need a guide, please to call on Zorzi!"

"We'll remember!" Nancy promised.

Inside the vestibule, Tara rang a bell under a small card bearing the name, *Sra. Angela Spinelli.*

Moments later, the ring was answered by a Venetian quite different from anyone either girl had expected. Nancy caught her breath and her heart skipped a beat as their eyes met.

The young man who had just opened the door was, beyond question, the most gorgeous man she had ever seen!

# 2

## A Shot in the Dark

The young man's hair was dark and curly, his eyes a rich greenish-amber. When he smiled—and he was smiling now as he regarded the two pretty girls standing on the doorstep—he revealed gleaming, even white teeth and a dimple at each corner of his mouth.

"*Si . . . ?*"

His questioning voice as he looked at them sounded, to Nancy's ears at least, as melodious as Luciano Pavarotti's. He was not quite as tall as the average movie hero—perhaps five-nine or five-ten, at most—but his slim figure was beautifully proportioned, with broad shoulders and narrow hips, and his chest and bare arms, revealed by his open-necked, short-sleeved knit shirt, were smoothly and gloriously muscled.

His smile gave way to a throaty chuckle, and Nancy became abruptly and embarrassingly aware that she had been staring at him, and so had her girl friend.

"Ah, *si! Ma certo!*" he exclaimed to Tara. "You must be Signorina Egan!"

"Y-y-yes, I am. And this is my . . . my friend, Nancy Drew."

A thrill ran through the teenager from River Heights as his lustrous eyes rested on her—for only a brief moment, but long enough to notice her attractive face and figure.

"Delighted to meet you both, Signorine! Please to come in!"

As he led the way from the tiled vestibule up a dark, well-worn flight of stairs, the young man went on, half turning as he spoke, "*Mi perdonate* for not introducing myself. I forget my manners. I am Giovanni Spinelli, but you must call me simply Gianni!"

He pronounced his nickname like "Zanni." Nancy suddenly realized that this was Venetian dialect, which meant that Zorzi's real name therefore was "Giorgio."

The stairway led to a second-floor apartment with a cluttered and disorderly, but cheerful, lived-in look. The furniture and carpeting seemed old and worn, but there were gay, colorful touches all about in

15

the form of batik drapes, oriental cushions, sculptured ornaments and wall paintings.

An attractive blond woman in her late thirties emerged from the kitchen in response to a volley of Italian from Gianni. As he gestured toward Tara, the woman rushed up to her and, with tears in her eyes, embraced the American girl emotionally. "Ah, *mia poverina!* To think that we must meet at last under such unhappy circumstances! I am Angela, of course, Angela Spinelli, your father's dear friend! He loved you so much and spoke of you so often and so fondly!"

It was obvious from the moisture glistening in her own eyes that Tara Egan was deeply moved. She introduced Nancy to Angela, who in turn explained that Gianni was her younger brother. She begged the American girls to join them in a meal of pasta, but upon learning that they had already lunched aboard the plane from Rome, she contented herself with serving them caffè espresso and dainty little almond-flavored Italian cookies.

"And now," Signora Spinelli said when her two visitors had been shown the proper hospitality, "I know that the time has come that we must talk about your father, my dear Tara, even though this will pain us both. No doubt you will wish to know the unhappy facts concerning his death."

Tara could only nod and bite her lower lip to keep it from trembling.

"What I can tell you will not take long," Angela

16

went on sadly. "Rolf, your father, was returning home late one night in a hired gondola. Suddenly a shot rang out from the *fondamenta,* one of the quays or stone curbs that they were passing. This is what the gondolier reported later to the police, you understand? He said the noise startled him, and he looked to see where it came from, so at first he did not notice what was happening to your father. But then, from the corner of his eye, he saw his passenger toppling overboard. As he turned in horror, he saw your father fall with a splash into the water!"

"B-but didn't he try to rescue Daddy?!" Tara exclaimed.

"Oh yes, of course, my dear! He rowed around and around, searching everywhere. But in the dark it was not easy to see, and although he spent much time looking, he says your father did not appear again above water."

Tara Egan burst into tears. Gianni, who had not taken a chair and was hovering about the room while the others conversed, rushed to comfort her.

"Please! Do not weep, Signorina! It is most painful to Angela and me to see you grieving so! Believe me, we are ready to do whatever we can to help!"

As he spoke, Gianni stroked Tara's arm and hand. Until now, the smiling, handsome young man had seemed so vain and cocksure that Nancy was startled by his sudden change of manner and his tender concern for Tara Egan.

17

Aloud, Nancy said cautiously. "May I too ask a question about Mr. Egan, Signora?"

Angela Spinelli flung out her hands. "*Ma naturalmente!* Of course you may ask, *cara!* You are a friend of Rolf Egan's daughter, and the two of you have come here together to learn what happened to him. What is it you wish to know?"

"Are we to understand that he was—shot to death?"

Angela shrugged her shoulders expressively. "As to that, who can say, my dear? The gondolier reported only that he heard a gun go off, or rather, what *sounded* like a gun going off. He cannot even be sure it *was* a shot."

"But if Daddy wasn't hit, why else would he have fallen overboard?!" Tara hastened to protest.

"Please do not be offended, *cara*, when I tell you that the gondolier said Rolf had been drinking *vino* that night, perhaps too much *vino*. The police say that he was probably tipsy and that is why he fell overboard. Or if there was, indeed, a shot, then the noise may have startled him and caused him to lose his balance—which, again, could explain why he fell into the water."

There was a sob in Signora Spinelli's voice as she spoke, and she dabbed her eyes with a handkerchief. Despite her rather operatic manner and gestures, Nancy sensed that she had loved Rolf Egan very much and was as deeply grieved over losing him as Tara.

"What did the gondolier see when he looked toward

the sound?" Nancy asked gently. "Could he make out anyone on the quay?"

"He is unsure of that, also. He *thinks* he may have noticed something move—as if, for instance, someone had darted into a passageway between two buildings. It could have been a gunman, perhaps. But his attention was distracted almost at once by his passenger falling into the water, so he had no chance to see clearly. Besides, it was very dark along the canal at the place where the accident occurred, and the only light came from the gondolier's own lantern."

"And Mr. Egan's body was never recovered?"

"Unfortunately not. The police assume that the current and tide carried it far out into the lagoon, perhaps even out to sea."

Tara was sobbing softly now, and Gianni continued to comfort her with pats on the shoulder. Angela Spinelli looked at them. Nancy could see that she was proud of her handsome young brother, and it was not hard to understand why. With his dark good looks and sleek athletic build, a good many Venetian girls and female tourists were no doubt attracted to him. Nancy realized her own gaze was continually straying in his direction, and she could feel a tingling warmth spreading through her whenever she let her eyes linger.

It's a good thing I won't be seeing too much of this fellow, she thought, or I could easily wind up being Female Victim Number nine hundred forty-seven!

Nevertheless, Nancy's feelings toward Gianni

weren't totally positive. There was a certain glitter in his luminous dark eyes, and a feline grace to his rippling muscular movements which seemed to hint that he could be as cruel and heartless as he was handsome.

Looking back at his sister, Nancy said, "Tell me, Signora, wh—"

"Please! You must call me Angela."

"Very well . . . Angela . . . what do *you* think happened to Tara's father? Did someone kill him?"

"Ah, *mamma mia!* How can you ask me such a terrible question?! I simply do not know!"

"Did he have any enemies? Was there anyone who might have wanted to harm him?"

This time Signora Spinelli took longer to answer. At last she shook her head. "No . . . none that I know of."

Yet Nancy, observing the expression that flickered over her face, strongly suspected that thoughts had just passed through Angela's mind that might well have some bearing on Rolf Egan's tragic mishap.

Tara, meanwhile, had stopped crying with a final convulsive sob. "Nancy's good at solving mysteries," she murmured tearfully. "In fact, in America, she's quite famous as a detective."

"*Èvvero?*" said Angela with a look of surprise. "Then perhaps one day she may be able to explain to us all this terrible thing that happened to your *caro padre!*"

But Signora Spinelli's voice sounded far from hopeful.

Nancy slipped an arm around Tara's shoulders and helped her pull herself together. Tara responded to her attentions and also flashed a grateful glance at Gianni. In return, the handsome Italian youth favored her with a dazzling smile calculated to melt the heart of any susceptible female.

"I . . . I suppose we'd better go over Daddy's personal effects." Tara asked.

"*Si,*" said Angela. "Perhaps now would be as good a time as any."

As they rose from their chairs, Gianni shifted his gaze from Tara and looked directly at Nancy. To her surprise, it was an arrogantly sensual glance—a smiling macho challenge, loaded with frank and open desire.

Nancy felt a nervous shiver pass through her. How could he look at her like that when just a moment ago he had been showing so much tenderness toward Tara? The vibes he was giving off seemed like a boast, almost a threat, that he could have any girl he wanted, whenever he cared to take her.

The boast or threat, whichever it was, left Nancy with a chill of mistrust.

Angela took Tara through the apartment, showing her Rolf Egan's belongings. They were surprisingly few—a limited wardrobe of clothing, a drawerful of personal papers including an envelope of snapshots taken over the years, and assorted art equipment, paintings and sketches.

Nancy, who had a keen artistic eye, found his canvases colorful and charming. They reflected Rolf's adventurous, bohemian spirit and certainly showed a good deal of talent. Yet she doubted that any of them would bring very high prices if exhibited at an art gallery. She privately concluded that Rolf Egan had been a gifted commercial artist, but not a creative genius.

As the two girls finished looking over his work, Angela clapped her hands and exclaimed to Tara with a smile, "Ah, *si!* Suddenly I remember now!"

"Remember what?"

"There is something your father wanted very much for you to have! In fact he was planning to send it to you just before his terrible accident! *Aspetta uno momento!* I shall go and get it!"

As she rushed off, Tara and Nancy exchanged curious glances, both intrigued by her words. *What special gift had Rolf Egan left his only daughter?* The two girls waited with keen interest to see what Angela would show them.

# 3

## The Watcher in the Shadows

To Tara's and Nancy's surprise, Signora Spinelli soon returned, carrying some bright-colored fabric. It proved to be a chef's apron with an attractive pictorial design in blue, yellow and green.

The design showed a figure in a chef's hat, flipping an egg in a skillet over the stove. Above this was scripted a motto in Italian: *Per fare una frittata, si deve spaccare un uovo!*

Angela Spinelli was watching Tara with a sympathetic smile. "No doubt you are wondering how your father came to give you such a thing," she said. "The answer is simple. Recently he was hired by a pottery firm in Milan to design a line of kitchenware to be sold in American department stores. Along with the dishes and bowls and cups, Rolf insisted the complete set

23

should also include an apron—and this is how he saw it. His client was delighted with the results! But do not ask me why he wished to send one to you."

"I think I know why," said Tara, and Nancy saw that her lashes were once again wet with tears. "Daddy used to *love* to play chef!"

"Ah, *si, cara!* You are so right!" exclaimed Angela. "Here in Italy, most men would be ashamed to take their wife's place in the kitchen. But Rolf *loved* to cook! His fettucini was exquisite and so were his American—how do you say?—*hamburgers!*"

Tara nodded and took out her handkerchief to dab her eyes while she went on, "I can still remember when I was little, before my parents were divorced, we'd have cookouts in the yard, at the summer cottage where we were staying. Daddy loved to put on an apron and a big old chef's hat while he prepared the meal—and then do funny things to make me laugh. . . . Somehow I knew the whole thing was a show he was putting on, just to amuse *me!*"

Her voice broke again, and she blew her nose to hide her emotion.

Nancy had learned a few words of Italian during an earlier trip abroad, but not enough to translate the motto. To give Tara time to regain her composure, she pointed to the lettering on the apron and asked curiously, "What does it say?"

"*To make an omelet, one must break an egg,*" Angela replied with a smile.

A faintly puzzled expression flickered over Tara's face. Then she sighed and gathered up the apron. "May I take this with me?"

"Of course, my dear. Rolf meant it for you."

"I'll come back later for the rest of the things."

"But, *cara*, why must you go?" Angela flung out her arms impulsively. "Surely you will stay here with me while you are in Venice! Gianni comes to visit and keep me company at times, now that Rolf is no longer here. But that is no problem! He can easily return to his regular quarters, so there will be plenty of room! To me you are like a daughter, *mia poverina*, surely you understand that?"

Tara hesitated uncertainly, and Nancy saw her eyes swing from Angela toward Gianni as her lips parted in a shy smile.

Gianni beamed a look of irresistible appeal at her, adding to his sister's plea. "Ah, *si!* Angela is right! You must certainly stay here with us . . . after all, you are like one of the family, *non è véro?* Please say that you will do so, Tara!"

Nancy could see her wavering. She could also imagine what was going through her friend's mind. If Tara stayed with Angela Spinelli, she was bound to see more of Angela's handsome young brother.

As she thought of Tara's unhappy home life and her obvious need for affection following the loss of her father, Nancy felt another sudden pang of mistrust. It would be so easy for a smooth, macho operator like

Gianni to take advantage of a girl in Tara's present situation and state of mind!

Even more disturbing were the mysterious circumstances surrounding her father's tragic accident . . . On the spur of the moment, Nancy spoke up before her friend could reply. "Tara has already checked into a *pensione*."

"But that is no matter!" said Angela. "I am sure they will let her check out again with no charge when they learn that Tara has been invited to stay with relatives."

Nancy looked doubtful. "Maybe, but she didn't just take the room today. It was reserved in Tara's name before she left New York. We'll see what they say," she went on smoothly. "Whatever happens, Tara will be coming back here for her father's belongings, and meanwhile she'll have to see about her own things at the *pensione*. There's no need to decide right this minute."

Angela glanced at Tara, who still looked hesitant but apparently was swayed by Nancy's words. "*Ebbene,* just as you wish, my dear," Angela said. "But please remember that you are always welcome here."

Nancy promptly moved toward the door. "Well, shall we be going then, Tara?"

"Y-yes . . . I guess we'd better."

"Let me come with you!" Gianni volunteered eagerly. "Then if Tara should decide to return to my sister's, I can assist with her luggage!"

There was no polite way to refuse.

As they went outside, Nancy's sharp eyes noticed a figure lurking on the other side of the *rio*, or side-street canal, on which Angela Spinelli's apartment was located. The man was standing in a shadowy passageway, so that it was impossible to make out much of his face or appearance, but she was sure she had glimpsed the same person standing there when she and Tara had arrived.

Gianni talked brightly and entertainingly as they made their way back over the quays and little bridges to the Pensione Dandolo. When they arrived, Nancy said to him with a smile, "Thanks so much for coming with us. And please tell your sister how much I enjoyed meeting her!"

"I shall be glad to wait until Tara decides what she wishes to do."

"No, thanks," she replied firmly. "We have some things to arrange, so we may be quite a while. If she does decide to stay with your sister, she can phone to let you know—right, Tara?"

"Uh, y-yes . . . I guess that makes sense."

"*Va bene*, let me give you Angela's number." Gianni wrote it down and handed it to Tara, then held the door of the *pensione* open for the two girls. "*Ciao* then, Signorine!"

As the girls entered the *pensione*, his lustrous amber-green eyes met Nancy's sapphire-blue ones for a moment. His bold smile seemed almost mocking, as if to say: *I can read you like a book, Nancy Drew! Don't think you can keep me away from Tara forever —or from you either, if I should decide that you are the one I want!*

Upstairs, in the comfortable but old-fashioned-looking bedroom Signora Dandolo had assigned to Tara, the blond girl exclaimed to Nancy: "Oh, my goodness! Isn't Gianni *gorgeous?!*"

"That's for sure. He's so handsome, I don't quite trust him."

"Is that why you stopped me from accepting Angela's invitation, because you thought he might make a pass at me?"

"Well, partly that, perhaps, but . . ." Nancy paused to marshal her thoughts. She was also wondering how to say most tactfully what was on her mind. "Tara, can you think of any reason why someone might have wanted to harm your dad?"

"No, not at all! That business about someone shooting at him sounds crazy! I'm sure Daddy never hurt anyone, at least not intentionally. So why should anyone want to hurt *him?*"

"If we could answer that, we'd probably know exactly what happened, but we can't and we don't," Nancy said ruefully. "That's what worries me, Tara. Let's just suppose some nut did want to shoot your father, for revenge or whatever. How do we know he may not try to hurt you too?"

Tara stared in amazement at the teenage sleuth. "Are you serious?"

Nancy shrugged drily, "Anything's possible." She went on to describe the faceless watcher she had seen lurking in the shadows, across the canal from Angela's flat.

Tara shivered. "That does sound a bit scary!"

"Then stay here, at least, overnight, and we'll talk some more tomorrow. Maybe the trouble just involves Angela, so if you're here at the *pensione*, you'll be in no danger."

"All right, if you say so. But what about you, Nancy?"

"I have to go on to a place called the Palazzo Falcone. My dad's expecting me there. It belongs to a wealthy Venetian who owns a glassworks on the island of Murano. Daddy's a lawyer, and he came here on behalf of a client who wants to buy the glassworks. But there's been a kidnaping that may affect the deal. That's why Daddy sent for me. He hopes maybe I can help solve the crime."

"Wow!"

Nancy's lips curved in a wry smile. "Yes, I know. Sounds pretty far out to me, too. But I'm willing to try."

"I bet you'll succeed, too!" declared Tara.

"Don't count on it. But that reminds me of something I wanted to ask you, Tara."

"Go ahead."

"When Angela translated that motto on the apron—you know, *To make an omelet, you have to break an egg*—it seemed to me you looked sort of puzzled for a second or two. Why?"

Tara gave a shrug. "Golly, I don't know exactly. It . . . it's just that . . . well, Daddy *hated* omelets. He never made them. In fact, I remember him saying once that the only people who made omelets were cooks who didn't know how to make nice fluffy scrambled eggs."

Nancy chuckled. "Sounds like my father. He and James Bond are both crazy about bacon and scrambled eggs. It's practically the only way Daddy will ever eat eggs."

"Why did you ask?" Tara inquired curiously.

It was Nancy's turn to shrug. "Search me. Whenever there's a mystery, I guess I'm always looking for clues, and one never knows where they'll turn up." She rose from her chair. "Well, I'd better get going, Tara," she said, "but I'll call you tomorrow, if not sooner."

Tara accompanied her downstairs to the parlor of the *pensione* and gave her an affectionate hug and kiss. Nancy asked Senora Dandolo if she could phone for a gondola or *motoscafo*, one of Venice's motorboat-taxis. The landlady said she could, but that it would be much quicker simply to walk a block or so to the Grand Canal and hail one.

Nancy had packed only a duffel bag and a light

30

suitcase for her trip to Venice, so she declined Tara's offer to help and started out alone for the Grand Canal.

She had gone only a few steps when she felt a hand on her shoulder. "*Scusi*, Signorina Drew! May I have a word with you?"

# 4

## Falcon Palace

Nancy paled, then felt a warm flush seep upward from her neck to her cheeks. She knew, without even turning around, who had spoken. It was Gianni Spinelli.

How handsome he looked as he strode up alongside her! He was the sort of guy, thought Nancy, whose physique would catch a girl's eye as quickly as his face would—both were devastatingly attractive.

Once again his smile played tricks with her heart. She tried not to notice the dimple at the corners of his mouth.

"What do you want?" Her voice sounded strained and unnatural to her ears.

"To walk with you, and talk with you. What else?"

As he spoke, he reached out to relieve her of her luggage. "Please! Let me carry those for you, Signorina! *Prego!*"

It seemed idiotic to resist or struggle with him on the street over such a matter. Nancy kept her duffel bag, which was slung over one shoulder, but allowed him to take her suitcase—even though she realized this provided him with the excuse he needed to accompany her.

"You were waiting outside for me all the while I was in the *pensione* with Tara?" Nancy inquired with a hint of exasperation, then immediately regretted asking. It sounded as though she were accusing him of some wrongdoing.

"As you see."

"Why?"

"*Cara!* Do you really have to ask?" With a dry little laugh, he looked deep into her eyes, as though at that moment there was no one else in the world but the two of them. "I waited because you are the most beautiful girl I have ever seen, and therefore I desire to be with you as often and for as long as I can! *E così*, does that answer satisfy you, Miss Nancy Drew?"

She tried to ignore what his words and his eyes were telling her, but it wasn't easy.

"How many other girls have you said that to?" she retorted, angry at herself for falling into his trap by asking.

"A good many," Gianni grinned and shrugged, "but this is the first time I ever meant it."

"From the way you acted at your sister's, I thought you'd fallen in love at first sight with Tara Egan," Nancy said tartly.

Gianni chuckled. "Do not worry, *cara*. You have no need to be jealous."

"*Jealous!*" Nancy gasped with indignation. "What on earth makes you think I'd be jealous of anyone you flirt with?"

"It was you who brought up the subject, my dear Nancy. Anyway, I assure you there is no reason at all to feel so. What I say or do with your little friend Tara means nothing. She is like a homeless puppy, grateful to anyone who shows her the least bit of attention or affection. The poor child does not even realize yet that she is a woman. She is ready to give her heart to any halfway attractive man who shows interest in her. Do you really think that I, Gianni Spinelli, could fall in love with such a *poverina*?"

He spoke with such smugness and preening vanity that Nancy was almost grateful to him. His words had just shocked her out of her fantasy and into her senses like a cold shower of reality, chilling her confused, romantic feelings. In a flash, they reawakened the mistrust she had felt back at Angela's apartment.

She thought of the warm adoring glances he had bestowed on Tara Egan, and the caressing way he had

34

stroked her arm and shoulder. Yet now, when Tara was not around, he talked about her in a contemptuous, patronizing way! There was no longer any doubt in Nancy's mind that Gianni Spinelli was just a calculating playboy whose only interest in the opposite sex was to gratify his own vanity. He would use girls for whatever he could get out of them.

His next words, breaking in on Nancy's thoughts, threatened to undo all her cool, logical reasoning. "With you, it is quite different, *cara*. You are an exciting, lovely woman who *knows* she is a woman and is not to be taken in by flattery or mere hand-kissing. To win your heart would be the proudest boast any man could hope to make!"

It was so cornily operatic a line that Nancy felt like laughing. The trouble was that when spoken by a hunk like Gianni, with those melting dark eyes, she found herself idiotically wanting to believe him, in spite of all her common sense!

By now they had reached the Grand Canal. Nancy was thankful that at that moment a gondola came steering up to the quay in response to her wave.

To her annoyance, Gianni stepped aboard with her.

"Where do you think you're going?" she asked bluntly.

"With you, Signorina Drew, if you permit," Gianni replied with a courtly air. (So now she was "Signorina Drew" again, instead of "Nancy" or *"cara"!)* "I wish

35

only to make sure you reach your destination safely. And on the way, perhaps you will allow me to act as your tour guide."

Nancy found it impossible to order him out of the gondola. It didn't seem worth making a scene about it in public so, with a shrug, she turned her back on him and gave directions to the gondolier.

As they glided out into the stream of water traffic, Nancy settled back on the cushioned passenger seat. For the first time since her arrival, she prepared to absorb and enjoy all the sights and sounds—and smells—of Venice.

Yes, the smell was certainly there—a dank, pervasive odor of canal water and distant salt air from the outlying marshes, faintly tainted with sewage—not too unpleasant, really. Like all tourists, Nancy quickly forgot such a trifling inconvenience when surrounded by the overwhelming charm of Venice herself.

The gondola was like a black swan, gliding gracefully along under the strokes of the gondolier in his striped jersey, sailor pants and black-ribboned straw hat. On either bank rose a fascinating array of architecture—domed churches, palaces, public buildings, and ancient dwelling houses.

In the bright summer sunshine under a cloudless blue sky, the brick and marble facades presented a rainbow of faded colors—raspberry, ochre, russet, pale lime and ivory, rose red and old gold. Loveliest of all, Nancy thought, were the *palazzi* with their columned arcades and small, delicate balconies and windows topped by pointed Moorish arches. The fact that many of the buildings were weather-stained and patched or crumbling seemed only to add to their charm. They looked as though they were floating on their own reflections mirrored in the canal.

For Nancy, the final enchanting touch was provided by the mooring posts, like striped barber poles, scattered along each bank.

Now and then the water was churned by passing *motoscafi* darting among the gondolas and barges and occasional *vaporetti*. Even a few rackety outboards intruded on the fairytale scene. Down the dark, narrow side-canals could be glimpsed small, picturesque humpbacked bridges.

"Venice is a very noisy city, I fear," Gianni was saying, as he pointed out the landmarks.

"Perhaps so, but it's a pleasant noise," Nancy mused aloud. Unlike the raucous din of New York's street traffic, the thrumming sounds on the Grand Canal were predominantly human, a medley of voices from the crowds swarming along the quays mingled with the shouted warnings of the gondoliers veering their craft out of each other's way.

Ever since they embarked, Gianni had kept up a stream of flirtatious remarks. Nancy managed to ignore most of them, but breathed an inner sigh of relief when the gondolier finally steered his boat toward the Left Bank to land, narrowly missing another gondola as he did so.

They had reached the Palazzo Falcone. Nancy recognized it at once from the fierce stone hawk jutting out like a gargoyle from a point high up on the facade. It obviously symbolized the family name of the palace's owners.

A flight of stone steps led up from the water to the arcaded front entrance, or loggia. Nancy shouldered her duffel bag, snatched up her suitcase before Gianni could take it, and stepped nimbly out of the boat onto the bottom step. Then she turned abruptly to pay the gondolier before her companion could disembark.

"Thank you, Gianni, for coming with me this far," she said coolly, "but I must say goodbye now. You'll understand, I'm sure, that I can't invite you in, since I'm only a visitor here myself."

Cutting short his plaintive response, she mounted the steps of the palazzo, suitcase in hand. The gondolier, grinning at Gianni's discomfort, was already rowing away.

Inside the columned stone porch, Nancy tugged a bellpull. Moments later, a cadaverous butler answered the door. He was wearing a dress suit that was shiny from long wear, and white gloves that looked none too clean. His long, bony horseface showed no expression whatever, and a patch over one eye gave him a villainous air.

"I'm Nancy Drew," said the teen from River Heights, somewhat intimidated by his manner. "I, uh, believe I'm expected."

The butler bowed in silence and stood aside while she entered. Then, after relieving her of her luggage, he led the way through a marble vestibule and a long dark hall to an ornate drawing room.

Her father, Carson Drew, rose from his chair with an eager smile. "Nancy dear, how good to see you!"

He strode toward her with outstretched arms, and they exchanged a hug and kiss. Then the tall, broad-shouldered attorney introduced her to the man with whom he had been speaking.

"Marchese, this is my daughter Nancy. Honey, this is our host, the Marquis del Falcone—or Marchese del Falcone, to give him his proper title in Italian."

Nancy made a mental note that his title rhymed with "Mark Daisy" and for the rest of the day kept thinking of their host by that name. I'll have to be careful not to call him that to his face! she thought, suppressing a smile.

The Marchese Francesco del Falcone was a courtly gentleman in his fifties, with dark wavy hair sprinkled with silver at the temples and a waxed mustache. In his beautifully tailored silk suit, with a sky-blue ascot at his throat and a carnation in his lapel, he looked every inch the aristocrat.

"Enchanted to meet you, my dear!" he said, pressing Nancy's fingers. "Your distinguished parent has

39

told me much about you, but even before now I had heard your name on one of my trips to America. It is my sincere hope that you may be able to help solve this unhappy kidnaping, which your father has no doubt told you about."

"I'll certainly do what I can," said Nancy, "though I'm sure your Italian police are already checking out every possible lead."

"*Si*, the *carabinieri* are quite skilled in dealing with such crimes. Unfortunately, kidnaping for ransom has become more and more frequent in Italy in recent years. But perhaps your own talent as a detective will suggest some new approach."

When they were all seated, Nancy said, "Tell me, please, about the person who was kidnaped."

"His name is Pietro Rinaldi. He is a master glassblower—the single most valuable employee of my glass factory on Murano."

"Forgive my ignorance, Marchese, but *why* is he so valuable?"

"Because he knows all the trade secrets that make our Venetian glass the finest in the world. In every factory on the island of Murano, there are expert craftsmen like Pietro, men whose skills have been passed down from father to son for generations. That is how Pietro became a master glassblower, by learning the craft from *his* father. My family, the Falcones, have owned our glassworks for over two hundred years, and all that time Pietro's family, the Rinaldis, has worked for us."

"In effect," interjected Carson Drew, "Pietro Rinaldi is one of the glassworks' main assets."

"So without him," said Nancy, "the company would be crippled, unless and until an equally skilled replacement could be found or trained?"

"Exactly. And in some ways, I gather, he could *never* be replaced, is that not so, Francesco?"

"*Si*, that is correct. Every Venetian glass factory, you see, has its own special secrets, and in the case of the Falcone glassworks, those secrets are stored mostly in the head of Pietro Rinaldi."

"Does he have any sons of his own?"

"Not yet. Pietro is still a young man, not much over thirty. As a boy, he ran away to sea and sailed all over the world. He even spent some time in your own country, living with his relatives in New Jersey. At first he planned to become a citizen and enlisted in the United States Marines. But later, when his father became seriously ill, Pietro had a change of heart. He returned home to Venice and applied himself seriously to learning all the secrets of glassmaking."

"How and when was he kidnaped?"

"Just three days ago, last Friday, to be precise. The police believe he was captured during the night in his house, probably at gunpoint. Next morning, I received an anonymous phone call from one of the gang

41

that snatched him. The caller told me Pietro was in their power and demanded one hundred thousand dollars in American currency for his safe release."

"Do you intend to pay the ransom?"

"Alas, that is difficult!" The Marchese del Falcone sighed and spread his hands unhappily. "The gang has given me ten days to pay the money, but I doubt if I can raise that much cash on such short notice. Times have been hard these past few years, and my family's fortunes have suffered. That is why I was planning to sell the glassworks to your father's client."

Nancy knew that her father represented an American firm called the Crystalia Glass Company and had come to Italy on the firm's behalf to negotiate the purchase of the Falcone glassworks. But Pietro's kidnaping had stalled the deal, since Crystalia believed the loss of the master glassblower could seriously hamper production at the Italian factory.

Carson Drew now explained that the Marchese had asked Crystalia Glass to advance him the hundred thousand dollars needed for the ransom, even before the purchase took place. "I've forwarded his request to my client. We're now waiting for an answer."

Nancy pondered for a few moments before asking, "What about the Italian police? I mean, what's their position on the ransom demand?"

"Officially they are against my paying it," replied the Marchese. "Privately they admit it may be the only way to save Pietro's life, since they have no real clues to go on in tracking down the criminals."

"Would it be possible for me to visit the Falcone glassworks, and talk to some of your employees?"

"*Si*, by all means! There is a young American there who will be glad to act as interpreter for you."

"I can take her over to Murano this afternoon," said Carson Drew. Then he glanced at his watch and added to Nancy, "The Marchese has a meeting scheduled with his bankers at two-thirty, to discuss ways of raising the ransom money, if my client won't help. It's almost that time now, Francesco."

"*Si*, they will be expecting me shortly. In any case, the two of you would no doubt enjoy some moments alone together, to chat personally. *E così*, if you will excuse me . . ."

With a smiling bow to Nancy, the Marchese del Falcone rose to his feet. "My butler Domenic will bring you some refreshment," he said as he left the drawing room. Mr. Drew turned to his daughter. "Well, honey, how was your flight over?"

"Very smooth and pleasant, Daddy. I even made a new friend." Nancy told him about Tara Egan and the fatal circumstances that had cost the life of Tara's father, Rolf Egan.

"How tragic!" Carson Drew exclaimed sympathetically. As they talked, the sinister-looking butler served them coffee, fruit and cheese.

"Where is Tara Egan staying, Nancy?"

43

"She's taken a room at a *pensione*. I hope to see her tomorrow. She still hasn't gotten over her father's death, and I'm a bit concerned about her. Do you suppose the Marchese would allow me to invite her here to the palazzo for tea?"

"Of course, I'm quite sure he would. Francesco's one of the kindest, most gracious hosts I've ever known."

When Nancy finished her coffee, Mr. Drew suggested that she might like to freshen up or lie down for half an hour before starting for the glassworks on Murano. Domenic showed her to her room.

After a brief but welcome rest, Nancy rose and ran some bath water. Then she opened her suitcase to pick out a change of clothing. Her eyes widened as she discovered a strange object inside—a fluted white shell she had never seen before!

Where on earth did that come from? she breathed half aloud.

# 5

## A Glass Menagerie

Nancy was both puzzled and intrigued as she picked up the sea shell for a closer look. She was quite sure it had not been in her suitcase when she went through Customs. But if she had not packed it, when and how did the shell get there?

The longest period of time the suitcase had been out of her sight since arriving in Venice was when it was left at the Pensione Dandolo, while she accompanied Tara to Angela Spinelli's apartment. Could someone have slipped in the shell during that time?

Why would anyone do such a thing? Was it related to the riddle of Rolf Egan's fatal mishap?

Nancy knew very little about sea shells, although she could recognize certain kinds. This one, she thought, was an Angel's Wing—a kind often found on Atlantic beaches back home.

Were they also found on the Adriatic shores of Italy?

Wait, I'm forgetting something! Another explanation for the shell had just occurred to Nancy.

She and Tara had passed through Italian Customs together after landing in Rome. Their luggage had been laid out on a long table. The inspection had been quick and courteous, but both girls had had their suitcases opened and poked through by the Customs officers.

Maybe the shell belongs to Tara, thought Nancy, and got dumped in my suitcase by mistake.

There was no time to fret over her odd discovery now. I'll ask Tara about it when I see her tomorrow, Nancy decided, and continued getting ready for the trip to Murano.

Minutes later, in a knit top and denim skirt, she hurried downstairs to join her father in the drawing room. To her surprise, Nancy found him chatting with a tall, graceful blond woman.

She had long-lashed eyes of delft blue and hair like spun gold. She was stunningly beautiful and reminded Nancy of a Renaissance angel in a painting by Botticelli she had once seen in a museum.

"My daughter, Nancy," Carson Drew announced proudly. "And this is Katrina van Holst, a Dutch photo-journalist. She has come all the way from

Amsterdam to photograph a masked ball that the Marchese will soon be giving here at the palazzo. You and I are invited, by the way."

"It is a great pleasure to meet you, Nancy," said Miss van Holst. "Carson has just been telling me all about you—boasting, in fact."

"Well, Daddy's a wee bit prejudiced," Nancy chuckled, "so you'd better take whatever he says with a grain of salt."

The three of them chatted for a while longer. Nancy found the Dutch woman witty and charming.

"She's a house guest of the Marchese, like us," Mr. Drew explained later as he and Nancy headed down the Grand Canal in a water-taxi. "And there may be one or two others, I believe, who'll be coming for the masked ball."

"Miss van Holst is certainly beautiful," said Nancy with a sidelong glance at her father.

He nodded. "Yes indeed, she's very attractive," then he changed the subject. "Nancy dear, would you mind very much if I don't come with you to the glassworks?"

"Of course not, Daddy, if you've other things to attend to. But you'll have to give me directions to Murano."

"I'll do better than that, honey. I'll put you on the boat to Murano, and I've already called ahead to have someone meet you."

47

Mr. Drew explained that he had received a telegram from his client while Nancy was resting. As a result, he had to wait at the palazzo for a phone conference later that afternoon.

"Who's the person I should look for when I get to Murano?" Nancy inquired.

"No problem. I gave him your description, so he'll be looking for *you*. He's that young American the Marchese spoke of, the one he said could translate for you if you wanted to question any of the employees."

"Oh, yes. What's his name?"

"Don Madison. Actually, he works for Crystalia Glass. Crystalia sent him over here about a year ago to learn the art of glassblowing from one of the Murano masters. In fact, that's what led to Crystalia's offer to buy the Falcone works."

Their motorboat turned up a *rio*, which led to a long, straight quay on the north side of Venice, called the *Fondamenta Nuove*. Nancy learned that *vaporetti* departed from here at regular intervals to Venice's smaller sister islands—Murano, Burano, and Torcello.

"Don't get off at the first stop on Murano," Mr. Drew warned her. "It's swarming with shills from every glass factory on the island. They shout themselves hoarse coaxing tourists to come to their particular exhibit, and then try to sell them everything in sight."

Nancy chuckled. "Okay, I'm warned."

The trip across the lagoon took only about twenty minutes. Nancy quickly spotted the young man who was to meet her. He was tall, rangy and sandy-haired. Something about his appearance instantly marked him as American. She felt she could have picked him out of a crowd, even if he hadn't come striding toward her as she stepped off the boat.

Thank goodness! thought Nancy. What a relief it will be to talk to an ordinary American guy again after fending off an exotic animal like Gianni!

This particular Yank might never make it as a magazine model, but there was a solid, homey, reliable air about him that, at the moment, seemed far more appealing.

His face had a lean, craggy, strong-jawed look that was far from handsome, yet attractive in its own way. Nancy could never have imagined him in evening clothes, or starring in a sophisticated movie. But she could easily picture him slouching on the pitcher's mound in a baseball uniform, straightening his cap and squinting at the batter just before winding up and firing a fast ball over the plate.

"Miss Drew?"

"Yes . . . and you must be Don Madison."

"Right." He turned away from the boat landing after the briefest of handshakes. "Plant's not far from here. Hope you don't mind walking."

"Not at all. I'll enjoy it."

Nancy was a bit put off by her escort's curtness. She hadn't expected a hometown welcoming committee, but she hadn't expected the cold shoulder, either. His official smile of greeting and the sizing-up look he gave her had seemed affable enough, at least for the length of their handshake. But did he have to turn quite so brusque and uptight the very next moment? He even seemed to be avoiding eye contact.

"I suppose my father told you why I've come to Murano?"

"Not really. Just something about you looking over the factory, maybe asking the hands some questions about Pietro."

Don Madison's tone sounded faintly disdainful, as if the thought of a girl her age snooping into a crime that baffled the police was too ridiculous to be taken seriously. Nancy realized that her father had probably told him as little as possible in order not to cramp her investigation.

"What are you, some kind of reporter?"

"No, some kind of detective, if you want to put it that way. I know it's pretty unusual and I don't look the part, but I *have* succeeded in other investigations."

Don flung her a sudden quizzical glance as they walked along. "Oh yeah, now it registers. So you're *that* Nancy Drew? . . . Sorry."

"It doesn't matter in the least," Nancy said coldly.

"I'll try not to take up any more of your time than I have to."

"Well, our production schedule *is* sort of messed up at the moment, now that Pietro's not around to keep things running smoothly."

Murano, too, it seemed, was an island of waterways, with a canal forming what appeared to be its main street. Don led the way through several alleys and turnoffs to a courtyard with a brick factory building at one end. A hawklike gargoyle and a sign over the doorway announced that this was the Falcone Glassworks, *Vetreria del Falcone*.

Inside, a balding man in a vest and shirtsleeves peered out at them from a cubbyhole office. Don Madison introduced him as Signor Rubini, the plant manager. He bowed obsequiously to Nancy and gabbled away in an accent she could hardly understand.

"Just a flunky," Don muttered as they walked on. "It's Pietro who really runs the plant—or *did* run it before he was kidnaped."

Glowing furnaces dazzled her eyes in the gritty, smoky production area. Fascinated, Nancy watched several husky, leather-aproned blowers at work as they dipped long hollow rods into the molten glass, then swung and twirled them to elongate the syrupy blobs. These were blown patiently into larger and larger translucent bubbles, with the workmen's cheeks puffing out like Dizzy Gillespie's, the jazz trumpeter. The result was then pinched, cut or rolled on marble tables to produce the desired end product —goblets, vases, bottles and figurines.

Don showed her how decorations could be formed by means of drops or lumps added from the outside, or by colored or milky threads embedded in the original glass.

"Do they often let visitors watch how these things are made?" Nancy inquired.

"What you've just seen is no big deal, these are all well-known techniques of glassmaking. The real secrets have to do with things like furnace temperatures and glass formulas."

Don explained that the early seafaring Venetians had learned the art of glassmaking from the Syrians and other peoples of the Eastern Mediterranean. Their glassware became the finest in the Western world and reached a peak of perfection in the sixteenth century, with the clearest crystal glass ever blown. But their know-how eventually leaked out to other countries of Europe, despite the best efforts of the Venetian secret police.

"You mean there was cloak-and-dagger espionage in the glass business, just like James Bond and the CIA have to fight off atomic or microelectronics spies nowadays?"

"There sure was. If a Venetian glassmaker defected to some other country, they'd either try to coax him back with bribes, or hire assassins to track him down and kill him."

Nancy shivered and wondered if any similar motives might be involved in Pietro's kidnaping.

Don's manner continued to seem rather gruff and unfriendly. Yet he helped her chat with the workmen in an offhand way, so that she would appear more like an inquisitive, young tourist than a snoopy private investigator.

One interesting fact Nancy noted was that Don Madison seemed to have been friendlier with the missing maestro than anyone else in the plant. Judging by remarks by both Don and the workmen, Pietro Rinaldi had evidently taken the young American under his wing, and the two had become close friends.

"Did Pietro seem worried over anything before the kidnaping occurred?" she inquired.

Don shook his head curtly. "Not at all."

"Did he have any particular friends outside the plant, or a girl friend, perhaps?"

"Not here in Italy. He's engaged to an American girl back in New Jersey. From the way he talked, I guessed he's been saving money so he can bring her over here in style next spring."

This reminded Nancy that she had no idea of what the kidnap victim looked like. "Was he ever photographed?" she asked Don.

"Not in a studio, if that's what you mean, but there's a colored snapshot of him and his girl."

"Where?"

"At his flat."

Nancy waited to see if Don might volunteer any further information, but none was forthcoming. The afternoon was almost over, and Nancy felt it was time to go before she outstayed her welcome. Before leaving, however, she asked if the Vetreria del Falcone had any glassware for sale.

"Tons of it. What would you like?"

"My aunt collects glass paperweights. She asked me to pick one out for her."

Don Madison led her to a storeroom, where a whole shelf filled with paperweights was on display. Their beauty was breathtaking. Seeing her interest, he relaxed enough to explain some of the patterns and technical terms, such as *millefiori*, garlands, swirls, crowns and mushrooms. A number of the weights contained lovely artificial flowers and butterflies. How the glassmaker had embedded them inside his work of art almost defied the imagination.

In the end, Nancy chose one that was simpler yet more subtle and unique—an oval paperweight filled with a swirling rainbow of colors. It was placed well back on the shelf, almost out of sight.

Don gave her a startled look of respect. "Not bad. You picked the best one of all. That was blown by Pietro himself."

Despite his protest, Nancy insisted on paying for it. Then her eyes fell on an enchanting display of glass animals. Don explained that they represented the mythological beasts of Venice.

"They're gorgeous!" Nancy murmured. "Did Pietro design these, too?"

"No, they were designed by an outside artist the firm hired, an American named Rolf Egan."

# 6

## *Unseen Eyes*

Rolf Egan! Nancy caught her breath.

A man had drowned or been shot to death under mysterious circumstances—and now his name had turned up in an entirely different context!

Was it just a coincidence?

Well, maybe, but Nancy had learned early on in her mystery-solving career to mistrust coincidences.

She came out of her thoughtful trance with a start as she realized Don Madison was observing her keenly.

"Did I say something wrong?" he inquired.

"Far from it," Nancy murmured. "Sorry if I seemed to be spinning my wheels. Actually, you just gave me something to think about."

She was pensive again for a moment before asking, "Where is Pietro's flat located, by the way?"

"Here on Murano, on the other side of the island."

"Will you be leaving the plant at closing time?"

"Nope, not for a while. We're going to shut down some of the furnaces. I've been acting as Pietro's assistant lately, so they expect me to oversee the job."

Nancy would have been glad to wait, had Don offered to show her Pietro's flat afterward. But he gave no sign of taking the hint, which left her no alternative but to thank him for his time and help, and say goodbye.

"Think you can find your way back to the boat landing?"

"I hope so. If not, I'm sure someone will direct me."

Weary and a trifle depressed, Nancy sailed back to Venice. Thoughts crowded her mind as she stood at the rail of the *vaporetto*. The lagoon was dotted with boats and its waters gleamed peacefully in the fading, late afternoon sun. A sleek white cruiseliner was rounding the eastern tip of Venice en route to the *Canale di San Marco*, where it would drop anchor.

What a day it had been, far more eventful than she'd ever expected! And now it was ending on a note of frustration. Nancy was conscious of a faint, lingering resentment toward Don Madison. Why hadn't he been more willing to help her follow through on her investigation of Pietro Rinaldi?

No, that's not fair, she chided herself. Who knew how long and sweaty a job he might have ahead of him at the plant? And when he did knock off, why should she expect him to put himself out for her sake?

All the same, she thought crossly, his manner might have been a little more gracious!

Getting off the *vaporetto*, she found a water-taxi to take her back to the palazzo. I wonder what the back of the palace is like? Nancy mused idly as they cruised along. Maybe this would be a good time to explore.

Her boatman-driver seemed to understand English quite well. When Nancy told him what she had in mind, he nodded. "No problem, Signorina. I show you how to get there."

Minutes later, he steered his *motoscafo* into a narrow side-canal and, after giving her detailed directions, let her off near one of the little humpbacked bridges. Nancy thanked him with a smile and a generous tip and started off on foot through an arched passageway facing the bridge.

It led her into a paved street, which widened into a broad, tree-shaded *campo*, or square. On one side of the square stood an ancient church; on the other, a grilled gateway.

The gateway opened into the courtyard of the Palazzo Falcone. It was a lovely spot filled with the fragrance of plants and flowering vines—clematis, rambling roses, oleander and honeysuckle. Crumbling statues added a picturesque touch.

Several people were seated on wrought-iron garden furniture in the flagstoned center of the courtyard. The Marchese and his guests were enjoying an aperitif in the open air.

"Welcome back, my dear!" said the Marchese. "Will you not join us?"

Nancy gratefully sat down and accepted a lemonade after a smiling exchange with her father and Katrina van Holst. She was also introduced to two new arrivals at the palazzo, Signor and Signora Gatti.

"Your visit to Murano was interesting, I trust?" her host inquired politely.

"Very much so. I even learned a little about glassmaking." Nancy displayed the rainbow-hued paperweight she had bought for her Aunt Eloise. "I also saw those beautiful mythological animals your plant is now producing."

"Ah, *si*, our Venetian bestiary! Marvelous creatures, are they not? We have great hopes for them in the export market, which is one reason why Signor Gatti is here, in addition to attending our masked ball."

Ezio Gatti was a bulky man with a sharp beak of a nose and beady eyes—rather sinister-looking, Nancy thought—but with a warm, jovial manner that totally belied his appearance. A successful exporter, he said he was already getting a flood of orders for the glass animals from American and European store buyers.

"How did you happen to pick the artist who designed them?" Nancy asked the Marchese.

"He was recommended by Pietro Rinaldi, and, as you saw, he proved an excellent choice. By the way, your father mentioned a girl friend you would like to invite here to tea. By all means do so, my dear! I am sure she will brighten the *Ca' Falcone*, as you and my other two beautiful lady guests are already doing!"

"Thanks ever so much. That's very kind of you!" Nancy wondered why her reference to the glass animal designer should lead him to speak of Tara. Did he know that she was the daughter of the artist, Rolf Egan? Or was it just a coincidence?

Aloud she asked, "May I call my friend now?"

"*Sicuramente!* My butler will show you to the phone."

"Perhaps I can help." Isabella Gatti rose from her garden chair with a smile. "Using our Italian phone system is not always easy for American visitors."

Signora Gatti accompanied Nancy into the palace. A slender woman with jet-black hair that set off her vivid coloring, she had on a chic afternoon dress that Nancy felt sure was a designer original. Her charming manner won her the teenager's immediate liking.

After looking up the number of the Pensione Dandolo, Mrs. Gatti dialed, and a rapid conversation in Italian followed, presumably with Signora Dandolo. Then she handed the receiver to Nancy.

"Your friend will be on the line in a moment."

"*Mille grazie!*"

"Ah, you are learning our beautiful language! Congratulations, my dear!" The signora walked off, beaming her approval.

Tara was delighted at being asked to tea at the palazzo and accepted happily. She was startled to learn that her father had been commissioned to design a set of glass animals for the Vetreria del Falcone. "What a strange coincidence!" she murmured.

"If it *is* a coincidence," was the response.

"Nancy, what do you mean?! You're not suggesting that that had anything to do with . . . with what happened to Daddy?"

"No, of course not. But if we could find out how he came to be chosen as the artist, it might shed a little more light on his work and what he was doing recently, which in turn might clue us in to whether anyone really did have a motive for trying to shoot him."

"Yes . . . I see what you mean." Tara's voice was thoughtful and troubled.

"One other thing. Were you by any chance carrying a sea shell in your luggage?"

"A *sea shell?* Why, no. What a funny question! Why do you ask?"

Nancy hesitated. "I'll explain tomorrow."

"Okay, see you then. And thanks for inviting me!"

Nancy changed for dinner, which was held in a magnificent dining room with dark beams, brightened by Renaissance murals. Over the seven-course meal, the Marchese described his plans for the upcoming masquerade ball.

"It must be a famous occasion, if Miss van Holst has come all the way from Amsterdam to photograph it," said Nancy.

Francesco del Falcone shrugged but smiled proudly. "It is certainly not the only Venetian *ballo in maschera,* but ours has been held by my family every year since the palazzo was built in 1595!"

"I'm sure Katrina's photos will do it full justice!" Carson Drew's remark earned him a dazzling smile from the beautiful Dutch woman.

Before retiring, Nancy decided to write a letter home to Hannah Gruen. The devoted housekeeper had cared for her like a mother ever since the untimely death of Mrs. Drew, when Nancy was only three.

Later, as Nancy sealed the letter, she glanced up from the antique rosewood desk just as someone was passing by in the corridor outside the sitting room. Her thoughts must have shown plainly on her face.

"'S'matter?" grinned Don Madison. "Surprised to see the hired help walking through the palace?"

"I . . . I guess you could put it that way," Nancy admitted, blushing with embarrassment.

Madison chuckled drily. "Actually, I live here."

"I'm sorry. I didn't realize you were a personal friend of the Marchese's."

"I'm not. Glassmakers have always ranked well up on the social scale in Venice. In olden times they were held virtual prisoners on Murano, but even so, they were allowed all sorts of special privileges. They could even marry into noble families."

The young American's smile took on a faintly sardonic tinge as he added, "Of course, I work for Crystalia Glass, which may soon buy out the Falcone works. I suppose that *may* have had a little bit to do with my being invited to stay here as a guest."

"What about Pietro Rinaldi?" Nancy inquired with sudden interest. "What sort of relationship did *he* have with the Marchese?"

"Well, maybe not quite like a father and son but, at least, say, an uncle and nephew. The two families have always been fairly close, I guess. Pietro often came here to the palace."

There was a brief silence before Nancy asked, "Did you have to work very late?"

Again Don Madison chuckled. "Late enough to miss dinner, but I grabbed a bite on the way. Why?"

His manner seemed friendly enough at that moment for Nancy to risk a rebuff. "Could you possibly take time tomorrow to show me Pietro's flat?"

"Sure, why not?" was the cheerful reply.

For some reason Nancy found herself looking forward with keen anticipation to her return trip to Murano. In fact, her mood the next morning was sufficiently buoyant that she decided to push her luck

63

and ask if she might go along with Don when he left the palace to go to work at the plant.

"Of course. Come on," he responded. He seemed more reserved than he had been the previous evening, but at least there was no sign of the brusqueness that had put Nancy off at their first meeting.

Maybe he's just shy, she thought. It was a surprising notion. Nancy found it rather pleasant.

As they chatted on the *vaporetto*, Don's manner seemed to thaw again. Once or twice, Nancy glanced sharply over her shoulder.

"Anything wrong?" he inquired.

"Not really." Nancy tried to shrug off his question with a smile. "I . . . I had a feeling someone was staring at me. . . . Probably my imagination."

"It'd be surprising if some guy *wasn't* staring at you," said Don. "You're very pretty."

Nancy felt her cheeks turning pink.

Don had to check in at the *vetreria,* but did not keep her waiting long. Once work was in full swing, he told the plant manager, Signor Rubini, where he was going and that he would return in an hour. Then he and Nancy set off on foot.

Along the island's shore, she could glimpse heaps of broken glass and other debris. Don noticed her glance. "You might not think so now," he commented, "but Murano was once a fashionable beauty spot. Rich people would come here to stroll in the gardens and chat with poets and artists."

Pietro's flat was located in a neighborhood where master glassmakers had long resided. Nancy was surprised that Don had a key.

"Pietro liked company," he explained. "Sometimes when he worked late, I'd bunk here overnight."

It was a typical bachelor's flat, comfortably if not very neatly furnished. Nancy saw no signs of a struggle. "What makes the police think he was kidnaped during the night?" she asked.

"Mostly because the lights were on when we came here looking for him the next day."

Don led the way to a scarred, wormholed desk and pointed out a photo. It was a framed, colored snapshot showing Pietro Rinaldi on the beach with his attractive American fiancee. Pietro was a strongly built, hairy-chested fellow with a likeable grin. Nancy guessed that the picture had been snapped somewhere on the Jersey shore.

"The Marchese says Pietro chose the artist who designed those glass animals," Nancy remarked. "Do you know why he picked Rolf Egan?"

"Well, Egan's a talented artist, of course . . . but they were old friends."

"Any idea where they met?"

"No, but they talked like old buddies. Could've been back in the States, I suppose."

"Did you know Rolf Egan had a fatal accident?"

Don Madison was startled on hearing the details. "Wow! Almost sounds like a Mafia hit, doesn't it?"

Nancy nodded, then stooped to pick up a playing card from the floor. It was lying face down by a wastebasket, as if someone had meant to throw it in but missed. It was the ace of diamonds.

"Any idea where this came from?"

Don shook his head. A search of the rooms failed to reveal any other cards.

The two walked back to the boat landing. The quay was crowded. Murano was already being overrun by its daily horde of tourists. Nancy realized that she and Don had scarcely spoken since leaving Pietro's flat. She stole a look at her companion and found him regarding her with a strange intensity.

The throng stirred into motion as a *vaporetto* approached. Nancy felt a sudden nudge in the small of her back. It was sharp enough to send her stumbling forward. She flung out an arm to grasp the protective railing, but the sudden jerky movement had caused her heel to break off, and she lost her balance.

With a cry of fear, Nancy toppled from the quay!

# 7

## Shell Game

Strong arms seized her as she teetered precariously on the barrier! In another moment she would have gone over and plunged head-first into the water!

Nancy's face was white, and her heart was pounding. It took a moment to collect herself. Suddenly she realized that her head was pressed against Don Madison's chest, and he was embracing her tightly as she clung to him.

"You okay?"

She nodded wordlessly, and there was a brief eye-to-eye communion before they separated. Nancy sensed a certain reluctance on both their parts to end the embrace.

"Looked like someone pushed you," Don said gruffly.

"Someone did. Then my right heel broke off and I lost my balance completely!"

They glanced around, but people were jostling past them to board the *vaporetto*. There was no chance now to identify the person responsible.

Suddenly Nancy remembered the prickly feeling she had had of someone watching her on the boat ride over to Murano. Was it possible that she'd been shadowed all the way from the palazzo?

If so, that push might have been no accident!

Nancy felt a chill of fear. Did someone want her dead? Or was she merely being warned? Maybe the intended message was that if she didn't stop her investigations, she might suffer the same fate as Rolf Egan!

"Sure you're all right?" Don had been watching her face and his expression showed real concern. He slipped an arm supportively around her waist.

Nancy smiled and nodded. "Quite sure. . . . Don't worry, Don, I'll be okay, aside from limping on one heel."

It was the first time she had called him by his first name. Don hesitated a moment and seemed to swallow hard. "How about staying on for lunch?" he blurted.

"I'd love to, but someone is expecting me back at the palace."

His face, which had lit up when she said "I'd love to," fell again at her mention of a previous date. But his smile returned when Nancy explained that a girl friend was coming for tea.

"Okay. See you tonight then, I hope."

"So do I. And thanks so much for taking me to Pietro's!"

"My pleasure. Believe me!"

On the *vaporetto*, sailing back to Venice, Nancy was warily conscious of everyone who came near her. She also took care not to stand too near the rail. Her thoughts kept reverting to that moment when she'd almost been pushed off the quay, only to be saved by Don Madison.

What a heart-stopping experience it had been! Yet oddly, now, she found herself enjoying the recollection . . .

Nancy had planned on having tea in the palace courtyard. But the sepulchral, eyepatched butler Domenic, who seemed to have a habit of doing exactly as he pleased, apparently felt that guests should be formally received in the drawing room.

*"Va bene, va bene,"* he had muttered when Nancy tried to make her wishes clear. But when Tara arrived, he proceeded to lay out the tea in the drawing room.

The old fraud, thought Nancy, smiling in spite of her irritation. He understands exactly as much English as he wants to!

Maybe the air-conditioned drawing room was a better place to have tea—if one didn't mind the lack of privacy. The afternoon sun was blazing, and the courtyard with its fragrant greenery was by no means free of insects.

Tara was entranced at the setting. "Wait'll I tell Mom about this!" she murmured breathlessly. "Imagine being invited to a Venetian palace!"

She was even more thrilled when the Marchese del Falcone looked in on the two girls and welcomed Tara personally. He seemed as taken with the shy, willowy blond girl as she was with him.

"Where are you staying in Venice, my dear?" he inquired. "At a *pensione?* But that is absurd! You must come here and attend our masquerade ball tomorrow night! Would you not like to have your friend as a fellow guest, Nancy?"

"That would be marvelous!"

"*Ebbene*, it is settled, then. I shall send a servant to the *pensione* to arrange matters and fetch your luggage."

Tara was overjoyed. But when she tried to express her gratitude, he merely smiled and brushed aside her thanks. "*Prego! Non c'è di che!*" he said, waving her imperiously to silence. "I beg you—it is nothing."

Mr. Drew strolled into the drawing room and was also introduced to Tara. "I'm so glad Nancy met someone her own age on the flight over," he remarked as they shook hands. "I'm sure it'll make her stay in Venice much more enjoyable."

"It's a break for me, too!" Tara declared, wholeheartedly.

70

The bellpull sounded in the central corridor. Moments later, Domenic entered the drawing room to announce a visitor. He handed the Marchese a card, and there was a rapid exchange in Venetian dialect. As the butler exited, Falcone turned to his guests.

"I have a caller, it seems, an Englishman named Oliver Joyce. An art collector, apparently. If you will excuse me, I shall go and see what he wants."

Before he could follow Domenic out of the room, however, the butler returned. With him was a tall, dapperly dressed man with a head that was shiny and bald, except for a wispy fringe of carrot-red hair.

"My dear Marchese," Oliver Joyce beamed, holding out his hand, "how kind of you to see me! I should have written first, but I was passing this way on the Grand Canal and decided to take a chance that I might find you at home!"

Joyce explained that he was not only a collector, but a dealer in objets-d'art. "I have heard that you may soon consider selling some of your family art treasures," he went on. "May I ask if these reports are correct?"

The Marchese smiled sadly. "An employee has been kidnaped, so it is necessary for me to raise a large ransom on short notice. I hope that my bankers may be able to arrange a loan on my family's olive groves and other land holdings. If not," he shrugged, "then our few remaining works of art may go on the block. . . . But not just yet."

Nevertheless, he graciously consented to show Mr. Joyce around the palace. Soon afterward, Carson Drew also left the drawing room to dictate some legal documents on tape to airmail back to his office in River Heights.

"By the way, Nancy," said Tara as the two girls resumed their interrupted tea, "you were going to tell me something about a shell."

"Yes, it was the strangest thing, Tara. When I unpacked yesterday, this is what I found in my suitcase . . ."

Nancy reached into her pocket and took out the white Angel's Wing.

Tara's eyes widened and her lips parted slightly. She sat very still, staring at the sea shell.

# 8

## A Sinister Sign

"What is it, Tara?" Nancy asked. "Is anything wrong?"

Tara shook her head silently without taking her eyes off the shell. She seemed to be having difficulty finding her voice.

Nancy explained, "When we went through Customs, I thought this might somehow have gotten transferred from your suitcase to mine. I mean, that maybe one of the inspection officers replaced it in the wrong bag, by mistake. . . . You say that's not the answer, though?"

"No. It couldn't have come from my suitcase."

"But you've seen this before?"

"Maybe not that particular shell, but one just like it." Tara reached out for the Angel's Wing and her hand closed around it almost fondly.

The teenage sleuth was intrigued. "Do you want to tell me about it?"

Tara's lips trembled and her eyes suddenly glistened with moisture. "Oh, Nancy, this is really unusual! Do you remember me telling you how my father once came to New York unexpectedly and took me to the Jersey beach, and how we sunned ourselves in the sand all afternoon?"

"Yes."

"I found a shell like this and gave it to Daddy. He told me he'd always carry it with him as a keepsake—to remind him of the fun we had that day!" Tara's voice broke emotionally.

Nancy was touched, but her instincts as a detective were also aroused. "You're sure this isn't the same shell?"

"How could it be? . . . Even if it were, there's no way I could tell for sure."

Nancy tactfully changed the subject, and the two girls were soon engaged in a lively conversation about their shopping and sightseeing plans. As they talked, Nancy saw Katrina van Holst passing by in the corridor.

"Come and join us," she invited, "if you can spare a few minutes."

The smiling Dutchwoman, who carried two cameras as well as a shoulder bag around her neck, came into the drawing room and was introduced to Tara Egan.

She accepted a cup of tea and sat down briefly to chat with the girls.

"Are you in Italy alone or with a group?" she asked Tara. On learning what had brought her from America, Miss van Holst sympathized warmly and expressed a hope that Tara might still take home pleasant memories of Venice, despite her father's tragic accident.

"Just visiting the Marchese's palace is something I'll never forget," said Tara. "And the masquerade ball sounds thrilling!"

Presently, after a brief tour of the palazzo's upper floors, the Marchese returned to the drawing room with his English caller. He showed the art dealer two oil paintings of Venetian scenes, then led him to a tall glass cabinet.

Nancy couldn't help noticing the keen, sidelong glances that Oliver Joyce kept casting in all directions while the Marchese was speaking. They seemed oddly out of key with his urbane, foppish manner and his show of peering intently through a monocle at whatever was being described. Nancy had a feeling that the Englishman's sharp eyes were recording every detail of the palace scene.

She also noticed something even odder about his right trouser leg, just above the ankle.

From inside the glass cabinet, the Marchese del Falcone took out a lovely Fabergé egg—one of the world-famous creations of Carl Peter Fabergé, court jeweler to the tsars of Russia. Jeweled and enameled in intricate designs, the eggs were intended as Easter gifts. Each contained a precious "surprise."

The one that the Marchese now opened contained a spectacular firebird with emerald eyes and ruby and diamond feathers. "My grand-uncle brought this back to Venice," said the Marchese. "He was at one time the Italian ambassador to Russia."

"Exquisite!" murmured Oliver Joyce. His awed tone was scarcely above a whisper.

Nancy, Tara and Katrina van Holst rose from their chairs to admire and exclaim over the gorgeous work of art.

Soon after Oliver Joyce departed with profuse thanks to the Marchese, Katrina also left the palazzo to photograph the sights of Venice for the magazine she was working for. Nancy showed Tara the palace courtyard with its blooming garden, and then took her up to her room.

On the way, Nancy excused herself momentarily for a private word with her father. She asked him to use his legal connections to find out if Interpol, the international police organization, had any information on Oliver Joyce.

"What do you suspect him of?" Carson Drew inquired with a quizzical frown.

Nancy hesitated. "Just possibly of casing the Palazzo

Falcone for a future robbery. Unless I'm mistaken, he was wearing a gun in a leg holster!"

Mr. Drew's face hardened and his frown deepened. "I'll see what I can find out," he promised.

Tara was entranced upon seeing Nancy's room. Its tall windows, curtained with brocaded draperies, opened onto a graceful little balcony overlooking the Grand Canal. Its wall paneling was intricately carved, and its ceiling decorated with small gilt plaster cupids. What caught her eye most of all were the two huge, canopied four-poster beds.

"Oh, Nancy!" she cried. "Why couldn't the two of us share this room? Would you mind?"

"Far from it. I was going to suggest the same thing myself."

"Then let's!"

There was a knock on the door. It was the eye-patched butler, Domenic. He announced that the two signorine had a visitor downstairs. "A young man who calls himself Gianni," he added disapprovingly.

Nancy sighed. "All right, thank you. Tell him we'll be down in a moment. . . . Oh, and Domenic, when Miss Egan's luggage arrives, will you have it brought to this room, please?"

"*Va bene.*"

Tara was obviously thrilled by Gianni Spinelli's visit. He looked more handsome than ever in an open-necked shirt and summer suit, with the cuffed sleeves of his jacket turned up halfway to the elbow.

77

He explained that he had gone to the Pensione Dandolo to invite Tara out on a short sightseeing tour of the city; but on learning from Signora Dandolo that she had gone to tea with a friend, he had followed her to the Palazzo Falcone.

"Perhaps you would care to come with us, Signorina Drew?" he added with an air of sleek assurance.

Nancy was about to decline coldly, when she was struck by a sudden pang of concern for Tara. The happy expression on her girl friend's face showed all too clearly how gratified she was at the prospect of a date with Gianni, and how eager she was to accept. Nancy also remembered Gianni's contemptuous remarks about Tara behind her back.

What kind of a friend would she be to leave her at the mercy of such a hypocritical wolf?

"Thank you, Gianni," Nancy replied with a cool, formal smile. "I'll be glad to come along . . . if you're sure three won't be a crowd?"

"Not at all! We shall be delighted to have your company, will we not, Tara?"

Tara's response was noticeably lukewarm.

Gianni had planned a gondola outing—with the girls no doubt paying the tab, Nancy reflected cynically. Considering the high fares, it would have been an expensive afternoon.

78

Instead, Nancy suggested that they leave by the courtyard and *campo* behind the palace and go on a walking tour of the island city.

Despite the heat of the afternoon, this turned out to be a happy inspiration. Following their noses, they strolled along narrow canals closed in on either side by high medieval buildings, over small bridges, through arching passageways and along flagstoned streets, glimpsing a side of Venice rarely seen by tourists.

In fact, the only typical tourist attraction spectacle the girls saw was a high pillared statue of a fierce-looking warrior on horseback—Bartolomeo Colleoni, once the mercenary commander of Venice's land forces. Nancy remembered reading somewhere that the splendid bronze figure, by Verocchio, was the greatest horseback statue ever sculpted. It was a thrilling sight.

The only flaw in the afternoon was the constant attention Gianni paid to Nancy. Once in a while he would bestow a grudging smile on Tara, or drop a flirtatious remark that brought an eager glow to her cheeks. But most of the time he would ignore her with a patronizing, macho arrogance, and speak flatteringly to Nancy or try to slip an arm around her waist.

Once, when they stopped in a little *trattoria* for some fruit ice, Gianni even reached across the table to caress Nancy's hand. She saw the hurt, unhappy look

79

that flickered over Tara's face and jerked her hand away as quickly and pointedly as she could.

Not long after passing the horseback statue, they came out onto the Fondamenta Nuove just as passengers were debarking from a steam launch. Among them, Nancy glimpsed Don Madison.

Her pulse raced and she found herself waving eagerly. "Don!"

Heads turned as the pretty strawberry blond called out his name. Don waved back and hurried toward them with a pleased grin. "Hey, what a nice surprise! What are you doing up this way, Nancy?"

"Seeing Venice—on foot," she chuckled, and introduced him to her two companions. Gianni's nostrils flared with ill-concealed dislike as he shook hands with the American.

"It's after five," Don remarked. "Going back to the palazzo?"

"We haven't decided yet," said Nancy. "So far we've just been wandering around, playing it by ear. Why?"

Don turned to Tara and Gianni. "Look, I hate to break up this happy trio, but would you mind very much if I snatched Nancy away from you?"

Tara certainly didn't. But Gianni looked sulky as Nancy smiled, "What did you have in mind?"

"Dinner. There uh . . . there are some things I

want to tell you about Pietro and the glassworks, things I've just remembered."

"Then we'd better talk, by all means." Nancy excused herself to her two companions, and Don promptly flagged a motorboat-taxi.

As they *put-putted* away down a *rio*, Nancy waved goodbye to Tara and Gianni. The handsome young Venetian watched sullenly and made no response. Tara, however, waved back with a happy smile as she clung to Gianni's arm.

"Was I rude?" said Don.

"Not in the least. And you couldn't have shown up at a better time," Nancy assured him.

Don took Nancy to a charming old inn, the Antica Locanda Montin, well off the tourist track in the Dorsoduro, a quiet residential area on the Right Bank, near the southern end of the Grand Canal. "My favorite eating place in Venice," said Don. "In fact, I had a room here before I was invited to stay at the palazzo."

The inn occupied a seventeenth-century building with a quaint lantern hanging over the front door. It was run by two brothers and favored by writers and artists, as indicated by paintings hanging on the walls. Don led the way to an inner courtyard where tables were arranged in a tree-shaded arbor. Nancy fell in love with the place at once.

"Do you really have something to tell me about

Pietro and the glassworks?" she asked when they were seated.

Don smiled sheepishly. "Not really. It was just an excuse to—to have you all to myself for the evening."

"I'm glad," Nancy said softly, and their eyes met. She knew at that moment that a new, wonderful relationship had begun. The attraction that had sprung up when Don had seized her in his arms to save her from falling into the lagoon was now flowing strongly between them.

Both began to talk at once, then broke off, laughing. "When we first met," Nancy confided, "I thought you didn't like me."

Don shook his head. "Far from it. I found you so attractive, it . . . it frightened me."

"Don't tell me you're all that bashful?"

"Not exactly. I intended to explain over dinner tonight, but now I suddenly seem to be losing my nerve again."

Nancy was puzzled, but she was enjoying their tète-â-tète too much to press him.

The dinner of *grigliata misti,* mixed seafood grill, was delicious, and dessert even more so—a mouthwatering wild-strawberry torte smothered with cream. Nancy reflected with a giggle that it would have sent her plump hometown girl friend, Bess Marvin, into swooning ecstasy!

Conversation ranged over all sorts of topics, including the Marchese's masquerade ball the following evening. "I'm going as a masked *bravo*, an old-time hit-man," Don chuckled. He recommended a shop where a wide assortment of costumes could be rented inexpensively.

Nancy was floating on a cloud when they returned to the palace. She went looking for her father and found him in a sitting room, listening as Katrina van Holst, seated at a piano, played a heart-melting Chopin sonata.

My goodness, Nancy thought with a gentle inward smile, are things getting serious?

"Well! We missed you at dinner, honey," Carson Drew remarked as she came into the room.

"I suspect she and Don didn't miss the rest of us in the least," Katrina added humorously.

Tara Egan was waiting in their room. She seemed in a contrary mood. Nancy gathered that Gianni Spinelli had taken her to dinner at some not very romantic spot, and that Tara was still feeling resentful over the afternoon's events.

"I don't understand you at all, Nancy!" she complained. "Are you in love with Gianni?"

Nancy was surprised that her own attitude hadn't seemed obvious. "Not at all," she declared. "Cross my heart, Tara!"

"Then why don't you stop playing games? You didn't *have* to come sightseeing with us!"

For the life of her, Nancy couldn't think how to reply. How could she possibly explain that she thought Tara was emotionally vulnerable and that Gianni was just a macho stud, out to exploit her longing for affection and romance?

In the end, she shrugged, "I'm sorry, Tara. From now on I'll try to stay out of the way."

Tara seemed mollified and ready to make up. Nevertheless, the bedtime atmosphere remained a trifle strained. Luckily Nancy was tired from her long, full day and quickly drifted off to sleep.

She was awakened some time later by a piercing scream. She jerked upright, striving to clear away the mists of sleep from her brain.

A faint sheen of moonlight was filtering into the room through the draperied windows—enough to reveal a dark something or someone in the center of the room.

Nancy's heart leapt to her mouth. She reached out in the gloom, groping for her bedside lamp, and switched it on.

A hooded figure was moving toward Tara's bed! It seemed to hear Nancy's stifled gasp and whirled around sharply.

Her eyes widened in horror as she saw a hideous skull face!

# 9

## Ghost Story

Nancy willed herself to leap out of bed and confront the ghastly intruder. But she was petrified with fright and her limbs refused to obey.

Another scream by Tara sent the weird phantom darting toward the doorway. It seemed to pause for just a moment, as if reluctant to be driven out by mere flesh-and-blood humans. Then as Nancy finally launched herself out of bed, it streaked into the corridor and the door closed behind it.

Nancy started in pursuit, only to stop short as Tara cried out fearfully, "Oh, my God—no! Don't go, Nancy! Don't leave me—*please!*"

She sounded hysterical. Nancy turned and hurried to her bedside and put her arms around the terrified girl. "It's all right, Tara! There's nothing to be afraid of! The spook's gone now, whatever it was!"

"Oh, N-N-Nancy! Did you see its face?"

"Yes. . . . I was hoping you hadn't," the teen sleuth added with wry humor, trying to relieve the tension.

"It was h-h-horrible!" declared Tara, shuddering. "When I woke up, that thing was coming toward me—and j-just for a second, the moonlight shone on its face! It was like a *skull!*"

The recollection brought on another spasm of weeping. Nancy held her close until the sobs died away. Then she rose from Tara's bedside and started toward the doorway.

"For heaven's sake, Nancy—be careful!"

She opened the door and looked out. The corridor was in semi-darkness, illumined only by the dim glow from a light in the gallery overlooking the ground floor. As Nancy's eyes adjusted, she peered intently in both directions, but there was no sign of the ghostly midnight marauder.

With a sigh of relief, she closed the door. "Whatever, or whoever, it was—is gone now!"

Apparently the inner walls of the old palazzo were solid enough to have muffled Tara's screams. They seemed not to have disturbed the household.

"What should we do, Nancy?"

"Good question. We could wake up the servants, I suppose, but I doubt if they'd appreciate it."

The two were feeling calmer now. In the end,

they settled back on their pillows and pulled up the covers. Tara kept her bedside light on as they chatted drowsily. Minutes later, both girls had fallen asleep.

Next morning, a maid brought them coffee and croissants. Tara tried to ask her if the palazzo was haunted, but the maid's English was too poor to carry on a conversation.

Soon after the girls finished dressing, there was a knock on the door. It was Domenic, the butler. "The maid, Eufemia," he grumbled in his hollow, heavily accented voice, "she say you see something last night."

"We certainly did," said Nancy.

Tara described the spook and repeated her question about the palazzo being haunted.

Domenic seemed both sullen and upset. "This is foolish talk," he scolded. "Only girls and women see any ghost."

"This wasn't just 'any ghost'," Nancy retorted. "We're talking about a terrifying figure that came into our room last night. Into *this* room right here!" She was determined not to let him evade the issue, as he had done yesterday afternoon when she wanted him to serve tea in the courtyard.

"*Si, si, capisco,*" Domenic nodded impatiently. "You tell me you see a ghost. What can I say?" He shrugged his bony shoulders. "This Palazzo Falcone, it is very old. Many times *donne* think they see something in the dark. Some see death's-head, like you say now. Maybe it is true, maybe they just imagine so. Who knows?"

The butler rambled on, shrugging and lapsing into Italian. The girls finally gave up. But on the way down to breakfast, they encountered the Marchese himself on the staircase.

"Is your palazzo haunted?" Nancy asked.

"Haunted?" The Marchese's face went blank. But when the girls described the apparition they had seen, and the butler's reaction to their story, he nodded understandingly. "Ah, *si*, the ghost! So Domenic has told you our old family legend, eh?"

"Not really. You mean the Palazzo Falcone has a legendary ghost?"

"Indeed it does." He explained that, centuries ago, a member of the Falcone family had been accused of plotting against the Doge, the elected head of the Most Serene Republic. So the dreaded Council of Ten, which controlled the secret police, had sentenced him to death.

The Falcones' kinsman was never seen again. It was assumed that he had been executed by the official strangler. But rumors persisted that he had been glimpsed at the palazzo, at first as a fugitive in hiding and later as a ghost with a death's-head.

Tara shuddered. "Are you saying that's what Nancy and I saw last night?"

"No, no, my dear, I'm only telling you the legend. I

am devastated that you have suffered such an unnerving experience, whatever the reason, and I apologize deeply. If it will help at all," he added, "I can assure you that there has never been any report of my restless ancestor harming anyone!"

The last remark was spoken with a sympathetic smile. Clearly, he was inclined to write off the weird specter as a figment of their imagination.

After breakfast the girls set out for a day of sightseeing and shopping. Nancy proposed that they go first to see the *Ca d'Oro*, or House of Gold. It had caught her eye when she arrived in Venice and seemed to her the loveliest palace on the Grand Canal. "The guidebook says it was built for a pair of wealthy newlyweds," she told Tara. "Once upon a time, it was actually covered with gold."

"Wow! They *must* have been rich!"

Viewed from the water, it looked as light and airy as a dream, with three stories of delicate columns and lacy arches. The girls entered on the land side, through a courtyard with a pink marble wellhead, and ascended a flight of stone stairs to the interior.

The palace was now a museum, filled with paintings and sculpture. As they wandered about, the two friends separated, each following her own interests. Tara became absorbed in a collection of doll-sized, bronze statuettes.

Nancy was looking for a picture by Titian, mentioned in the guidebook. Her interest in this artist's work had first been mere curiosity, prompted by hearing her own red-gold hair described as "titian." But the more of his paintings she saw, the more she had come to admire his vivid use of color, which had revolutionized the art of the High Renaissance.

The particular work of Titian in the Ca d'Oro was a voluptuous painting of Venus decked with pearls. How magnificent! What artistry! Nancy marveled. For that matter, what a woman! she mentally added, with an admiring twinkle.

"Her hair is almost as beautiful as yours, eh?" said a masculine voice behind her.

Nancy turned coldly, vexed at the way the spell had been broken, and even more vexed by the fact that the speaker was Gianni Spinelli.

"What are you doing here?" she snapped.

"The same thing you are doing, *cara*—worshiping beauty."

"Please! Spare me your corny line!" Nancy retorted, tight-lipped. "You've been seeing too many movies."

"Movie stars no longer turn me on," Gianni said softly, "now that I have seen *you* . . . !"

Nancy felt angry and helpless, all the more so since she couldn't help thinking how handsome he looked with his curly dark hair, finely chiseled features and muscular grace.

Gianni seemed to sense what was going through her mind. He smiled confidently and took a step toward her.

He must have followed us here, Nancy realized, and just waited for a chance like this!

The thought of being spied on by someone like Gianni filled her with distaste. And what if Tara should walk into the room and find them together, especially after her jealous outburst the night before!

"Please go away," she said aloud.

Instead he came a step closer. She could smell his masculine scent and the fragrance of his after-shave cologne. A panicky feeling of weakness assailed her.

Suddenly he seized her in his arms and kissed her! For a moment Nancy was too shocked to resist—and perhaps part of her responded to the warmth of his lips on hers.

Then fury and sheer indignation took over. She broke free of his embrace and slapped him hard. Her sapphire eyes were blazing.

"Leave me alone," she warned between her teeth, "or I'll call a guard!"

Gianni's face went as white as her own, except for the reddish imprint of her hand on his cheek. "So, you are in love with that American *grullo* from the glass factory!" he muttered in a voice thick with rage.

Then he turned abruptly and walked out of the room. Nancy was trembling.

Luckily she had recovered her poise by the time Tara rejoined her. But the encounter with Gianni had spoiled her pleasure in their tour of the House of Gold.

Tara was eager to window-shop, so after leaving the Ca d'Oro the girls caught a water bus to the Rialto. This famous covered bridge over the Grand Canal was lined with a double arcade of shops. Goods of all kinds were on display—jewelry, fabrics, glassware, shoes, lingerie, linens—every possible item, it seemed, to tempt the buyer. Tara was unable to pass up a gaily embroidered peasant blouse. Nancy bought a sleek pair of leather gloves for Hannah and an elegant silk tie for her father.

As they made their way down the marble steps on the eastern side of the bridge, Nancy felt a slight tug on her shoulder bag. She glanced around quickly, but in the swarming crowd, it was impossible to tell who might have snatched at it in passing, or even whether it had been done on purpose.

Then she saw what had caused the tug.

A folded slip of paper was tucked under the flap of her bag!

# 10

## Rendezvous with Danger

Nancy's pulse was racing. She opened the paper as they walked along. It bore a hastily penned note:

> *Meet me on Piazzetta at 6:00*
> *under Winged Lion.*
> *A Friend of R's*

Beneath the message, the sender had drawn a four-cornered lozenge—the shape of a diamond in a pack of playing cards.

"What's the matter?" said Tara, who had noticed Nancy's sudden odd behavior.

"I'll explain later." Nancy smiled as calmly as she could. "Hungry enough for lunch?"

"Starved!"

"Let's find a place to eat, then."

With the Rialto behind them, they were now walking down the Merceria, Venice's main shopping street. It was lined on both sides with shops and stalls, but these were plentifully interspersed with restaurants, *trattorias*, *caffes*, *gelaterias*, *rosticcerias*, and eating places of all kinds.

The girls chose a terraced outdoor cafe and settled themselves at a pleasant little table under a striped umbrella. Nancy had planned to confine herself to a salad, but was unable to resist the luscious-looking *canneloni* that Tara ordered. By the time they had finished lunch, topped off with a dessert of lemon sherbet and chocolate sauce, both girls felt sated.

"Whew! I could sit here for the rest of the afternoon," said Tara.

"Likewise. But don't forget, we still have to find costumes for the masked ball tonight."

"Oh, that's right! Any idea where to go?"

"Yes, Don Madison recommended a place . . . right here on the Merceria, in fact." Nancy fumbled in her bag for the address.

"That reminds me. What was that paper you were frowning over just as we left the Rialto—some kind of note?"

Nancy nodded and reluctantly showed her friend the pink slip. Tara's eyes widened as she read it. "Hey, what's this all about?"

"Someone slipped it under the flap of my bag. Now you know as much as I do."

"I don't get it." Tara looked bewildered. "What does this 'Friend of R's' mean, for instance?"

"Good question. The R could stand for the last name of the kidnaped glassblower, Pietro Rinaldi . . . or it might even refer to your father's first name, Rolf."

Her words seemed to electrify Tara. "Oh, Nancy!" she gasped. "Do you really think that's possible?"

The teen sleuth shrugged. "There's one way to find out."

"You mean—you're going to keep the appointment?"

"How else can I find out?"

"But, Nancy, what if it's dangerous? I mean, my dad was shot or drowned, and another man's been kidnaped. What if someone wants *you* out of the way, too, just because you're trying to solve those crimes?!"

The same thought had occurred to Nancy, especially when she recalled her frightening experience on the boat landing on Murano. Nevertheless, she tried to reassure her friend. "St. Mark's Square is the most popular tourist spot in Venice, Tara. No one would dare try to harm me right out in public! Now come on, let's go find that costumer Don told me about."

The shop was farther along the Merceria. Its windows were crammed with costumes of all nationalities and periods, as well as masks and falsefaces. As the two girls stood looking at the colorful display, a familiar voice suddenly spoke.

*"Buon giorno, Signorine!"*

Nancy's heart sank. It was Gianni Spinelli again! Tara's face lit up eagerly as she turned to greet the handsome young Venetian. But Nancy felt a surge of anger. How dare he show his face again, after what had happened just a few hours earlier at the Ca d'Oro!

Tara began chattering away about how they had come to pick out costumes for the masquerade ball which the Marchese del Falcone was giving tonight at his palazzo.

"May I come in with you?" asked Gianni. "Perhaps I can help by translating, if the shop owner does not understand English."

"Oh, wonderful! We'd love that, wouldn't we, Nancy?"

The titian-haired teen responded with a cool smile which didn't reach her eyes. Much to her satisfaction, the shop owner spoke English fluently. When Nancy told him why they had come, and that his shop had been recommended by Don Madison, the plump, mustachioed costumer exclaimed, "Ah, *si! Ma certo!* I was just about to wrap his costume and send it to the Palazzo Falcone!"

He showed them a dashing eighteenth-century getup featuring a plumed hat, cloak and rapier. "He will go as a deadly swordsman, you see? An assassin—

of female hearts, no doubt!" The costumer twirled his mustache and tittered appreciatively at his own wit.

After long discussion and the trying on of various costumes, Tara finally chose the gown and headdress of a medieval princess, while Nancy decided to be an Oriental dancing girl. The proprietor promised to send their selections promptly to the palazzo, along with Don Madison's costume.

When they left the shop, Gianni excused himself. He said he had an urgent assignment to cover for his work as an aspiring news reporter. Nancy had noticed a tiny miniature camera tucked in his coat pocket. She thought it was more likely he was a *paparazzo*, the kind of photographer who pesters celebrities and tries to snap sensational photos of them, which he can sell for high prices. But she was too pleased and relieved by his departure to give the matter a second thought.

The afternoon was well along, but the high point of the day's sightseeing still lay ahead at the southern end of the Merceria. This was the world-famous square called Piazza San Marco, which Napoleon had once called "the drawing room of Europe." It was framed on three sides by arcaded buildings with shops and cafes, and on the fourth by the Basilica of St. Mark's. As always, the huge square was thronged with tourists and strollers. A tall bell tower overlooked the scene, while pigeons flocked overhead or alighted boldly on the mosaic pavement.

Nancy decided at first sight that the Basilica, with

97

its five Oriental domes, was the most gorgeous and exotic church she'd ever seen. Over its doorway pranced four beautiful bronze horses brought home as loot from the pillage of Constantinople.

On entering, the interior seemed bathed in a golden glow from the Byzantine mosaics glittering in the vaulted cupolas overhead. The golden altarpiece was studded with precious stones.

One corner of the Piazza opened onto a smaller square, or Piazzetta, leading down to the waterfront, with the pink marble palace of the Doges on one side. The girls had scarcely an hour to view its splendid halls and treasures of art. Nancy made up her mind to return again for a more leisurely inspection before leaving Venice.

When they emerged, it was a quarter to six. "Oh, Nancy! Are you sure you want to keep that appointment?" Tara fretted anxiously.

"Of course I'm sure. Now you go back to the palazzo and tell Daddy I shan't be long."

Two towering columns overlooked the mole, or jetty. One bore a statue of Venice's original patron saint, Theodore, standing oddly triumphant over a crocodile. The other was topped by the unforgettable Winged Lion of St. Mark's.

Nancy saw Tara aboard a *motoscafo*. Then she settled herself on the round base of the lion column. From there she could gaze out over the harbor, where the Grand Canal joined the lagoon.

There was no telling, of course, from which direction her contact might come. Nancy's keen eyes scanned the Piazzetta. Minutes passed. Presently she heard the giant mechanical figures on the square's clock tower strike six gongs.

Once again Nancy's gaze swept the scene. Her pulse quickened as a stocky man in safari garb came walking toward her. He had a scarred, deeply tanned face, and his lips twitched in a flickering smile of identification. She knew this was him.

But suddenly he seemed to freeze. His smile changed to a snarl of anger. Without a word to Nancy, he turned and hurried away!

# 11

## Secret Search

Nancy sprang to her feet in dismay. She was sure the khaki-clad stranger had been coming to speak to her. But something had frightened him off!

There was no use going after him now. He was already disappearing into the crowd. Pursuit might only convince him that she'd tried to turn their rendezvous into a trap.

Another figure suddenly caught Nancy's eye, that of a dark-haired, handsome young man.

*Gianni Spinelli!* He was strolling toward her with a faintly mocking smile on his lips.

Nancy suddenly clued in and fumed in frustration. So that's who alarmed the mystery man and spoiled everything! Nancy was furious. The grinning idiot! He'd just wrecked her chance of learning something important—maybe a clue that would have unlocked the whole mystery!

"Are you following me again?"

"*Cara!* How can you talk to me like that?"

He was mocking her, getting back for the way she had slapped him at the Ca d'Oro.

Nancy's jaw clenched. Why waste words on such a vain creep! Slipping past his outstretched hand, she headed for the Grand Canal. Minutes later, she was riding back to the palazzo in a water-taxi.

As the boat cruised along, she put Gianni out of her mind and concentrated on the mystery man.

Thinking over what had just happened, she sensed something about him that seemed strangely familiar. But what was it? . . . Surely not his face. With his bone-deep tan and that livid scar running at an angle from the corner of one eye down across his cheek, he was altogether too distinctive. Nancy had trained herself to be observant and remember faces. If she'd seen him somewhere before, even just glimpsed him in a crowd, Nancy felt instinctively that his features would have lingered in her memory. As it was, they rang no bells.

Wait a minute . . . something stirred at the back of her mind. *A figure in the shadows . . .*

Suddenly Nancy remembered! A man had been lurking across the canal when she and Tara and Gianni had come out of Angela Spinelli's apartment. She hadn't seen him clearly enough to make out any details, but wasn't his general appearance somewhat like that of the mystery man who had tried to meet her just now under the lion column?!

That must be it, Nancy concluded.

Arriving at the palace, she paid her boatman and scampered up to the loggia. She was still a bit uncertain whether courtesy required her to use the bellpull or simply walk in.

The problem was solved when Domenic opened the door. He must have seen her arriving.

"Is Signorina Egan here?" Nancy inquired.

"*Si.*" The cadaverous butler jerked his head upward in the general direction of their room.

Nancy mounted the graceful staircase. A glance at her wristwatch showed that it was just six-thirty. I wonder if our costumes got here okay, she thought. I should've asked Domenic.

Their room lay well down the corridor from the gallery. Nancy opened the door—and stopped short in consternation.

The room had been ransacked! Both girls' luggage had been unpacked by a maid soon after their arrival and arranged neatly in the drawers of a big old *cassetone*. But now the drawers had been yanked out and clothing scattered all over. Several of the drawers were still hanging open.

The wardrobe, too, had obviously been searched. Dresses had been pulled from their hangers.

Tara sat huddled in a chair, her face pale and frightened.

"Good night! What happened?" said Nancy.

"Search me." Tara shrugged helplessly. "It was like this when I got back."

"Have you told anyone yet?"

"No. It was so scary and upsetting, I . . . I didn't know *what* to do! Besides, I was afraid of messing up clues or evidence."

"What about our costumes? Have they arrived?"

"Yes." Tara indicated two boxes on her bed. "They must have come just before I got back. They were still in the downstairs hall, so I brought them up myself."

Nancy dropped her parcels containing the gifts she had purchased on her bed and sat down to collect herself. Tara had mentioned clues, but there were certainly none in plain sight.

With a sigh, Nancy rose and began wandering about the room, straightening up at random while she tried to marshal her thoughts.

Obviously the marauder had been searching for something, but what?

"Did you check your belongings to see if anything's missing?" she asked Tara.

"Yes, and nothing's gone as far as I can tell."

"What about money or valuables?"

"My money's mostly in traveler's checks, and I was carrying those with me, in my purse. Other than that, and this ring and watch I'm wearing, I didn't bring anything very valuable."

"What about things belonging to your father, or *pertaining* to your father?"

Tara looked startled. "I'm not sure I know what you mean. I didn't bring anything of Daddy's to Italy with me—I mean, no official documents or identification. There's that apron, of course, that Angela gave me . . ."

"Is it still here?"

"Yes, in that top drawer that's hanging open."

Nancy walked to the window, drew aside the draperies and gazed down pensively at the Grand Canal. Rightly or wrongly, the intruder must have *thought* she or Tara had something valuable or important . . . why else the search?

Wait a sec, Nancy reflected. What about that spook who scared the wits out of us—was he looking for something too? Is that why he came sneaking into our room in the middle of the night?

Maybe he'd paid them another visit! It had obviously been a hasty visit, too frantic and hurried to put things back in place, probably because he feared they might return at any moment.

This reminded Nancy of the way the "Friend of R's" had been alarmed and left when he spotted Gianni. She'd known at once that he'd seen someone when his gaze turned away from her. . . .

Suddenly a thought flashed through Nancy's mind.

The spook must have spotted something, too—
something important. Of course! That's why he'd
paused just before fleeing out the door!

But what had he seen?

Nancy walked quickly to the door and tried to
repeat the actions of the skull-faced spook.

"What are you doing?" Tara asked curiously.

"Trying an experiment." Let's see now, Nancy
thought, he was sort of looking off to the right—which
meant that his gaze would have been directed toward
the . . . toward the dressing table!

Something on the dressing table must have caught
his eye.

Like what . . . ?

The rainbow paperweight!—the souvenir she'd
bought on Murano for Aunt Eloise's collection. That
*had* to be the answer! There was nothing else of value
on the table, just the girls' toilet articles and cosmet-
ics.

Nancy confided her idea about the paperweight to
Tara, who looked relieved and slightly confused.

"Gee, it's beautiful, but I didn't realize it was so
valuable! How much did you pay for it, Nancy, if you
don't mind my asking?"

The teen sleuth chuckled, "No fortune, or I couldn't
have bought it!"

If correct, Nancy realized, her deduction proved
something else—namely that last night's skull-faced
phantom was *not* the same intruder who had ran-

sacked their room this afternoon. Otherwise the rainbow paperweight would now be gone.

In a cautious afterthought, she tucked the oval glass weight into the toe of one of her shoes, which seemed a safe temporary hiding place.

Feeling better because of her brief exercise in detection, Nancy glanced at her watch. "It's past seven!" she cried. "We'd better hurry up and get ready for the masked ball!"

# 12

## Masquerade

An hour or two later, the two girls descended the main staircase of the palazzo in costume. Tara looked appropriately romantic and graceful as a princess of the Renaissance. Nancy felt wickedly exotic in her gauzy Arabian Nights garb as a dancing girl. Both wore silver domino masks, but Nancy had realized too late that her costume provided no way of disguising her telltale red-golden tresses. She had no intention, however, of letting such a trifling oversight spoil her enjoyment of the evening.

Both girls giggled as their staircase appearance was greeted by wolf whistles and applause.

The *ballo in maschera* was soon in full swing. Lights blazed out across the Grand Canal from the windows of the Palazzo Falcone, and its carved portals stood wide open for the arriving guests. Gondolas could be seen drawing up to the palace steps by the glow of lanterns bobbing from the striped mooring poles and floodlights on the loggia.

Inside, pageboys in powdered perukes and knee breeches wove about among the guests, offering trays of refreshments. Two groups of musicians were alternately filling the air with their strains. In the drawing room, a medieval trio in colorful hose and doublets were performing on lute, harpsichord and oboe. The girls strolled separately to the marble-floored ballroom with its splendid vaulted ceiling and chandeliers, where a rock band was waiting its turn to play.

Nancy's heart lifted as she saw who was coming in from the balcony terrace overlooking the courtyard—a cloaked figure with a plumed hat and basket-hilted rapier. It was Don Madison in his costume as an eighteenth-century *bravo!*

Just as he reached her side, the players broke into their own unique Venetian form of rock. Don swept her into his arms and they danced out across the floor. Nancy surrendered willingly to his lead; she could feel the beat pulsing in her blood. Somehow she'd hardly expected such a serious, reserved type as Don Madison to be quite so exuberant a dancer!

He was whirling her out toward the starlit privacy of the terrace, but even before they passed through the open glass doors, his arm was drawing her toward him in a closer, more passionate embrace—and now his lips were moving toward hers.

It was her masked partner's height that struck the first false note in Nancy's mind. She recalled the way her head had rested against Don's chest when he saved her from falling off the quay. Now, somehow, there seemed to be less difference in their respective heights, which was all the odder since he was wearing high-heeled boots.

As they kissed, the scent of his cologne tingled her nostrils. At the same moment, Nancy saw a tendril of hair that had escaped from under the bandanna tied around his head under the plumed hat—not a sandy curl, but a jet-black one!

With a gasp, Nancy pushed him away. "You're not Don!" she blurted. "You're *Gianni Spinelli!*"

The *bravo* released her gracefully and raised his mask. "Right, my dear Nancy! What a clever little detective you are!" Dimples were showing at each corner of his mouth.

His smile infuriated her, but she strove to stay calm. "You're the clever one, it seems! How did you manage it, Gianni?"

"It was very simple, *cara.* I returned to the costume shop soon after you left and picked out something for myself—a cowboy costume, like Clint Eastwood, you know?" Gianni chuckled, "in one of our, how do you call them?—'spaghetti westerns'! The shop owner remembered seeing me with you and Tara, of course, so when I offered to deliver the costumes to the palazzo, he was happy to accept!"

"And, of course, you *kept* Don's costume, and switched labels on the boxes so that he got yours?"

"*Esattamente!* And do not tell me that you did not enjoy my kiss just now!" Still grinning at his own cleverness, Gianni suddenly pulled Nancy toward him and kissed her again.

She stiffened in revulsion. Her voice remained ice cold as he released her and she stepped back from his embrace. "If we weren't at the Marchese's party, I'd slap you for that—as hard as I slapped you at the Ca d'Oro. But I don't want to make a scene. Now leave! Or must I call the servants and have you thrown out as a gate-crasher!"

For a fleeting instant, Gianni's grin faltered and his expression hardened vindictively. A second later he was his handsome, smiling self again. He touched his fingers to his lips and threw Nancy a jaunty parting kiss. Then he turned and strode off across the balcony terrace into the darkness.

Nancy started back into the ballroom. Her nerves were on edge. She was just in time to see a tall, sandy-haired figure in western gear turn and walk rapidly away. He had a poncho on his shoulders and a sombrero on his head.

Oh, no! Nancy wailed inwardly. That was Don— and he must have seen everything! And misinterpreted everything—the two embraces, Gianni's triumphant smile, the parting kiss! A wave of despair swept over her. I've got to go after him and try to explain! she thought frantically.

But Don wasn't the only person who had witnessed her encounter with Gianni. A blond girl, dressed like a medieval princess, was also watching. Despite her silver mask, the stricken expression on her face was all too apparent.

"Please don't think what you're thinking, Tara!" Nancy begged as the two girls came together. "You can have Gianni! I don't want him. I detest him, in fact!"

"What difference does it make? He doesn't want *me!*" Tara's words came out in a choking sob.

She turned away, only to bump into a masked pirate, who seized her merrily and whirled her off across the marble dance floor to the throbbing strains of Venetian rock.

Nancy watched helplessly for a moment, then hurried in pursuit of Don. She found him snatching a glass of champagne from a passing tray.

"Don, listen to me!" Nancy begged. "It wasn't at all like you think! Let me tell you what really happened!"

He shrugged indifferently. "I *saw* what really happened. I've got eyes. So what? You don't have to apologize to me if some guy turns you on."

"Gianni *doesn't* turn me on! You've got everything

all wrong, Don! I want you to understand what happened! Won't you please let me explain?"

"Don't bother. It's not all that important."

"It *is* important! Aren't you even interested in hearing what I have to say?"

"Not especially. I've got other things on my mind."

Nancy's shoulders drooped as he walked off, glass in hand. Her heart was pounding. The masquerade ball had started out as such fun! Why, oh why, did things have to turn out like this?!

Nancy clenched her fists till her nails dug into her palms. She had hurt two of the three people in Venice whom she cared about the most—unintentionally, perhaps, but deeply, all the same. At that moment she felt like rushing up to her room, flinging herself on the bed and sobbing her eyes out!

But something, nature, or childhood discipline, had given a steely streak to Nancy's character. It went too much against the grain to give up or feel sorry for herself. She squared her shoulders, choked back the sobs that rose in her throat and lifted her chin.

Minutes later she was dancing with her father, her feelings under tight control. He was made up, not very convincingly, like a Chinese mandarin.

"When did you get back from Murano, Daddy?" Nancy asked, making conversation.

"Around four—and I've been on the phone most of the time since then. I barely had time to get ready for the ball."

112

"You make a striking mandarin!"

"Thanks. That peekaboo costume of yours is quite eye-catching too, sweetie."

Nancy chuckled. A flashbulb blazed somewhere across the room, one of the many she had seen since the party began. "Where's Katrina? Taking pictures?"

"I imagine so, though I haven't seen her yet. She told me she was coming as a Dresden shepherdess."

"Sounds perfect with that lovely golden hair of hers."

A buffet meal was being served in the dining room. Presently the Drews joined other guests lining up for the tempting repast. Nancy's eyes roved about the crowded room, suddenly settling on a tall man dressed like a comic-hall British empire-builder in white ducks and tropical pith-helmet.

He had just spilled a crumb of food from his plate. As he bent forward to flick it from his clothing, a monocle slipped out of an upper pocket and dangled on its chain.

*Oliver Joyce!* Or was the monocle just part of his masquerade costume?

He looked somewhat like Joyce, though his mask made it hard to be sure; nor could Nancy see his hair color, due to the neck cloth dangling from his pith helmet. And the helmet itself made an effective cover-up of baldness.

What about a leg-holster? There were too many

people in the way to see whether he was wearing shorts or full-length trousers.

Before Nancy could shift position for a better view, the man handed his plate to a servant and left the room.

"Excuse me, Daddy," said Nancy. "I'll be right back!"

Giving up her place in line, and side-stepping other guests, she hurried after the comic-hall Britisher. But once out of the dining room, she paused. Which way had he gone?

Nancy walked along the center hall, peering into every room. A finger tapped her on the shoulder. "Excuse me, Miss Drew . . ."

She swung around, startled. The speaker was a man in a Harlequin clown costume, with a funny-looking long-nosed falseface. "May I have a word with you—in private?"

"Who are you?" Nancy asked cautiously.

"A friend of R's." The man turned and headed in the opposite direction, beckoning her to follow.

He paused in the doorway of a room which was evidently empty. Nancy joined him, and they entered the room together.

"May I see your face?" she said.

He pulled aside his mask, revealing a tanned, scarred visage—the face of the man she had seen just a few hours earlier on the Piazzetta!

They eyed each other in silence for a moment. Then Nancy murmured, "All right, thank you. What is it you want to see me about?"

Before he could answer, the lights suddenly went out. *The whole palazzo was plunged into darkness!*

# 13

## Dark Deeds

Nancy froze momentarily in fear. Had she walked into a trap?!

But the mystery man's voice spoke reassuringly. "Don't be alarmed. I'm not going to hurt you. I didn't arrange this blackout. It must be an accident."

He had a faint guttural accent that Nancy couldn't place—not Italian or French or Spanish—German, maybe, or some kind of Central European.

A hush had fallen over the crowd of party guests when the lights went out. But now Nancy could hear a babble of voices rising in the corridor.

"Who are you?" Nancy asked.

"Call me Hans. My full name does not matter."

"All right, go ahead. I came here as you asked, so tell me whatever it is you have to tell me."

"Your girl friend, Tara Egan, may be in great danger! Keep an eye on her at all times!"

"Danger from whom—or what?" Nancy probed. "Can't you tell me any more than that?"

There was no answer.

"You say you're a friend of R's, but *which* R? Pietro Rinaldi or Rolf Egan?"

The silence continued. Nancy suddenly realized that Hans was gone. She reached out in the darkness, groping in all directions, but her fingers met only thin air.

Annoyed at her own lack of vigilance, Nancy turned back toward the doorway. Tiny flickers of light were appearing here and there as guests snapped cigarette lighters or struck matches.

Presently she heard the Marchese's voice speaking somewhere in the hall, first in Italian, then in English. "My friends, I regret most deeply this inconvenience. But it will not be for long, so please remain calm. My servants are now doing their best to restore the lights, and in case there is any special problem, I have also telephoned for an electrician. In the meantime, please make yourselves as comfortable as you can. Candles are being fetched, so there should soon be at least *some* light. A thousand thanks for your patience!"

He had barely finished speaking when the lights suddenly blazed back on! Guests blinked in the sudden dazzling brilliance and burst into loud chatter.

The original level of music, noise and general merriment was quickly restored.

Nancy made her way to the ballroom and was much relieved when she saw Tara dancing with the young man in the pirate costume. Then she went looking for her father and found him in the dining room, holding two plates of food.

"Thank goodness!" Carson Drew exclaimed. "It's foolish of me, I know, but I was beginning to get a bit worried, honey. Let's find a place to sit down and enjoy this food. It looks quite delicious!"

As they ate, Nancy told him about the tanned, scarfaced mystery man called Hans, and the warning he had just given her about Tara Egan. "I'm afraid Tara's a bit put out at me just now, Daddy," she went on, "so would you sort of keep watch on her?"

"Of course. No problem. But who is this mystery man, Nancy? Any idea?"

"A friend of *both* Pietro Rinaldi and Rolf Egan, I suspect. And he *may* be a South African."

"What makes you think so?"

"Just a wild hunch, to be honest." Nancy explained what had put the idea in her mind. The note he had slipped her on the Rialto bore a diamond design—which in turn reminded her of the ace of diamonds she had seen at Pietro's flat—and both in turn made her think of real diamonds, for which South Africa is known.

"Also, he spoke with a slight accent that I couldn't place," Nancy went on. "But many of the South African whites speak a language called Afrikaans, which I've heard is based on Dutch, and that might very well fit his accent."

When she was through eating, Nancy went from room to room of the palazzo, making a hasty survey of the guests, but failed to sight either of the two she was looking for. Unless they had changed costume, she guessed that they must have slipped away from the palace during the blackout.

This would not be surprising in Hans's case. Since their rendezvous had been interrupted, he had come in disguise to warn Nancy that Tara was in danger—having delivered this warning, he'd left.

But what about the pith-helmeted Britisher? Was he really Oliver Joyce? And if so, what was he doing at the masquerade ball?

Nancy's eyes suddenly widened and she slapped her forehead. "What an idiot, I am!" she gasped.

She hurried to the drawing room and looked in the glass cabinet. *The Fabergé egg was gone!*

The Marchese, when notified, took the news with surprising calm. "*Ebbene,*" he said with a resigned shrug. "I suppose we had better check all the Falcone art treasures, so we can give the police a complete list of what is missing."

Nancy waited with the Marchese in his study for the outcome of the check. Twenty minutes later Domenic came walking into the room. Nancy was startled to see that the eyepatched, cadaverous butler was holding the Fabergé egg!

It was unharmed but open, and the lovely little jeweled firebird was gone. Nancy was even more surprised when the Marchese burst out laughing.

"But the firebird—!" she started to protest.

"No great loss, my dear. The jewels were mere glass. I pawned the real firebird several years ago when I needed money, and at that time I had a cheap copy made for the sake of appearances!"

It turned out that a servant had spotted the empty egg lying in a wastebasket, a fact which intrigued Nancy. The egg alone was fairly valuable, but apparently the thief had been interested only in its *contents*. None of the other artwork in the palace was missing.

At midnight the guests removed their masks and the festivities reached their peak. Tara was still with the young man in the pirate costume, but Don Madison was nowhere in sight. The butler told Nancy he had retired for the night.

Later, in their room, Nancy found Tara in cheerful spirits. "I'm sorry I made such a fuss about Gianni," the blond girl apologized. "Right now, I don't care if I ever see him again!"

Nancy smiled. "So I gathered from the way you and that fellow in the pirate costume seemed to be enjoying yourselves."

"Oh yes, isn't he terrific! His name's Kevin, and he lives in Connecticut. We've made a date to go hiking when we get back to the States!"

Obviously Gianni Spinelli was all in the past as far as Tara was concerned.

Nancy was pensive as she got ready for bed. She had a feeling that pieces of the puzzle were beginning to fall into place, but there were still many things that she didn't understand.

"Tara, you told me your father was adventurous and traveled all over the world," Nancy finally remarked aloud. "Was he ever in Africa?"

"Hmm . . . I don't believe he ever told me so, as far as I can recall. But I think he *must* have been, in North Africa, anyhow."

"Why? What makes you think so?"

"Because I have a picture of him, and it looks like it might have been taken in Egypt or Morocco—someplace like that."

Tara opened her purse and took out a snapshot encased in plastic. It showed two men, one in a U.S. Marine Corps uniform. They were grinning and standing together in what looked like a Middle Eastern open-air bazaar.

The civilian, blond and bearded, bore an obvious resemblance to Tara.

Nancy felt a quiet surge of excitement. "Do you know who the marine is?" she asked softly.

"No. Who?"

"Pietro Rinaldi!"

Yawning and weary, the two girls snuggled down in bed. Nancy fell asleep almost as soon as her head hit the pillow.

She was awakened by a voice screaming across the room. It was Tara, screaming as fearfully as she had done the night before!

Nancy sat bolt upright. In the semi-darkness, she could make out a figure moving across the room. She reached out to turn on the light, but in her haste knocked over the bedside lamp. It crashed loudly to the floor!

The noise, however, had at least one good effect: it seemed to shock Tara to her senses. She stopped screaming and switched on her own lamp. Just as the room brightened, the door slammed behind the retreating figure.

Nancy didn't hesitate. She sprang out of bed and started in pursuit, only to stumble over the lamp. She dropped to one knee, straightened up again, flung on a robe and dashed out the door.

The gallery light was off, and the corridor lay in darkness, but Nancy could dimly glimpse the intruder. She raced after him. Muffled sounds indicated that other guests had been awakened.

Seconds later she reached the stairway. Footsteps echoed below. She stopped short as she heard the door of the palazzo open and slam!

Nancy hurried back to her room. Tara stared at her,

wide-eyed and trembling. Without a word, Nancy rushed to the window, drew back the draperies and stared down at the moonlit canal. A dark figure had just untied a gondola from its mooring pole in front of the palazzo and was pushing off.

Nancy let go the draperies and turned back to her friend. "Tell me what happened!"

"The ghost wh-wh-whispered my name!" gasped Tara. "And look—!" She pointed to the floor.

Wet footprints were visible on the carpet!

# 14

## Game Plan

Tara's eyes were still wide with fear and shock. Nancy put her arms around the stricken girl and murmured gently, "Whatever it was that came into our room, Tara, it's gone now! There's nothing to be afraid of, believe me!"

Soon Nancy hoped, she might be able to provide a full solution to the mystery, backed up by evidence and proof. But for now, all she could offer was words of comfort. Reliving what had just happened or nit-picking over the details would just reawaken Tara's fears and upset her more than ever.

"Y-y-you're right," the blond girl agreed shakily. "Ghost or not, worrying about it won't help any, I guess . . . and it certainly won't bring Daddy back!"

Under Nancy's soothing influence, Tara gradually settled back on her pillow and became calmer. Meanwhile, Nancy's own mind was busily processing the available data and trying to compute the most logical explanation that would cover all the facts.

"Remember yesterday afternoon when we ran into Don Madison coming back from Murano?" Nancy said presently.

Tara nodded. "What about it?"

"When you got back here to the palazzo, did you stop and chat with anyone, or just come straight up to our room?"

"I came straight to our room."

"You didn't speak to anyone, or mention that I was out with Don?"

"No. Why?"

Nancy smiled and patted her friend's hand. "Just trying to fit together a few more pieces of the jigsaw puzzle, that's all."

As she returned to her own bed, Nancy reflected. If Tara said nothing, how did Katrina van Holst find out I spent the evening with Don? Who else but Tara would have known—*unless I was followed!*

It was a disturbing notion, well worth checking into, Nancy decided. Gradually she drifted off to sleep again.

Next morning Nancy awoke brimming with energy. She had made up her mind overnight to press ahead

125

for a solution to the mystery, actively setting events in motion, rather than waiting passively for clues to turn up. A plan was already taking shape in her mind.

A number of guests had stayed on after the ball, and the breakfast table was humming with conversation. After a quick bite to eat, Nancy quietly arranged to have coffee with her father in his room.

"Any report from Interpol yet, Dad?" she asked.

"Yes, I had a call from Paris this morning. You were right, Nancy. Oliver Joyce does have a criminal record as a jewel thief and art swindler. The Italian police have already picked him up for questioning, but he doesn't have the bird from the Fabergé egg."

"Someone beat him to it, I suspect. What's the latest word on the kidnapping and the ransom?"

"My client, Crystalia Glass, is willing to put up half the ransom money if the Marchese can provide the rest. He's agreed to that, and his bankers are willing to advance him a loan. The police chief here in Venice, Commandante Manin, is coming to the palace this afternoon to put his okay on the plan."

"Great! Do you suppose I could sit in on the meeting, Dad?"

"Why not? You came here to help."

Nancy quickly explained what she had in mind. Mr. Drew was enthusiastic. Then she spoke in turn to the Marchese, to Isabella Gatti and to Tara. All fell in with her plan willingly.

Presently Tara and Signora Gatti set out in the

Gattis' luxurious motor cruiser, heading first for Angela Spinelli's flat to invite her along for the day's outing, and then for the great domed church of Santa Maria della Salute at the southern end of the Grand Canal. Their instructions were to act like typical sightseers, but to wait at the church for a squad of plainclothes officers of the *Sicurezza,* the government security force, who would arrive soon afterward and stay with them as a protective escort until further notice.

Meanwhile, broad hints were dropped to the servants that a sensational break in the kidnaping case was near. By the time the police chief arrived, the whole palazzo was humming with excitement.

At the outset, Commandante Manin of the carabinieri was none too cooperative. A burly, hard-eyed cop who had coped with many terrorists, he had little faith in any plan put forward by a mere slip of a girl—even one with the mystery-solving reputation of Nancy Drew. But as she talked, his eyes warmed, and he finally broke into an appreciative chuckle. "You are a clever little fox, Signorina Drew! Something tells me these kidnapers may soon regret the day they were foolish enough to match wits with you!"

When the meeting was over, everyone walked out of the room with an air of suppressed excitement and confident good humor—a fact duly noted by everyone else at the palazzo.

Nancy sat down and dashed off a note to Tara, which she tucked in the edge of their dressing table mirror where it would be plainly seen by anyone entering the room.

> Dear Tara,
>
> Hang onto your hat and get ready for some exciting developments!
> The police have just had an incredibly lucky break—they expect to close in on the kidnapers' hideout within 24 hours!
> I've found out the crooks are after something that's worth a fortune, and Pietro Rinaldi knows all about it.
> Once he's free, he'll lead us right to it! He also knows what *really* happened to your Dad!! See you soon!
>
> Bye now,
>
> Nancy

She also jotted another note, hand-lettering the words with a bolder, thicker-tipped pen.

**TONIGHT IS THE DATE WE AGREED TO GET TOGETHER BEFORE I HAD TO CLEAR OUT OF VENICE AND LIE LOW, REMEMBER? I'LL MEET YOU AT MIDNIGHT WHERE WE PLANNED, AND YOU'LL HAND IT OVER TO ME. DON'T DOUBLECROSS ME, OR YOU KNOW WHAT'LL HAPPEN TO YOU!**

**HANS**

When she finished, Nancy tucked the letter in an envelope which she addressed to:

**PIETRO RINALDI**
**VETRERIA FALCONE**
**MURANO**

Then she changed to jeans and a cotton top, repaired her makeup and kissed her father goodbye. Outside, on the palace loggia, she hailed a passing water-taxi which took her to the Pensione Dandolo. As she walked in, she was greeted happily by the Signora's little boy.

"Hi, Zorzi!" Nancy replied. "You're just the person I'm looking for!" She took a five-dollar bill from her purse and held it up for him to see. "Would you like to earn this by running an errand for me?"

"*Si! Si*, Signorina!" Zorzi exclaimed, his eyes as big as saucers.

"All right, I want you to deliver this letter for me to a certain glass factory on Murano—and of course I'll pay your boat fare over and back, besides the five dollars. But you must listen carefully and do exactly as I say!"

Zorzi listened intently, then nodded. "Okay! I do just like you tell me!"

Leaving the *pensione,* Nancy went next to the charming old inn, the Antica Locanda Montin, where Don had taken her to dinner. She sat down at a table

129

under the arbor and ordered tea. Twenty minutes later, Don Madison arrived.

His steps slowed as he approached, and he stood waiting for her to speak.

"Can we be friends, Don?" said Nancy. Her heart was thumping, and she felt unexpectedly nervous.

There was a moment of silence before he replied, "I guess that depends on whether or not you can forgive me for acting like such an idiot last night."

Nancy relaxed, and they both broke into smiles. Don sat down, facing her across the table. Suddenly the atmosphere between them was as though the previous night's painful episode had never occurred. He reached across the table and they clasped hands happily.

"So now you're going to tell me what this is all about?" said Don. "The Marchese just called me at the plant and said I was to leave work early and meet you here. All very hush-hush and top-secret. No explanation."

Nancy proceeded to fill him in, while Don listened with keen interest. Presently he ordered wine and antipasto, and they went on talking while they ate.

"All right, now run the whole thing by me once again," Don said after Nancy had answered most of his questions.

"It's still just a theory, remember, but try this for size. Number one—Rolf Egan and Pietro were old buddies. Somewhere, quite a while back, maybe in North Africa, they met a man called Hans and cooked up some kind of secret deal with him."

Don nodded. "Check."

"Number two—as a result of this deal, they wound up in possession of something very valuable or important, which I'll call *The Prize*. Unfortunately they also wound up in big trouble with some dangerous crooks, because these crooks want The Prize for themselves— in fact, they're even willing to commit murder to get hold of it."

"So it seems."

"Now for a key question," Nancy went on. "Where *is* The Prize? My hunch is that Hans brought it to Venice, and the crooks trailed him here. Hans then turned The Prize over to Rolf Egan and lit out for parts unknown, maybe hoping to lead the crooks astray on a false scent. But his ploy didn't work. The crooks stayed put in Venice and went after Rolf Egan."

Again Don nodded. "To be precise, they took a shot at him one night, and he fell into the canal."

"Right! Which left them still without any answers to that all-important key question," said Nancy, "namely, where's The Prize? So they turned their attention to the one remaining partner in the deal, Pietro Rinaldi."

"But wait a minute," Don frowned. "We've been

131

assuming all along that Pietro was kidnaped for ransom . . ."

"Because that's what the crooks *want* us to assume," said Nancy. "But if my theory's correct, the real reason they kidnaped him was to extract information about The Prize. The ransom was just an extra bet on the side. Or maybe call it an insurance policy—a guarantee that whatever happens, their project won't wind up a total loss. In other words, if they can't get the information they're after, they can always sell Pietro back to the Falcone Glassworks for a hundred thousand dollars."

"Yeah, I see what you mean," Don mused. "Neat trick if they can pull it off."

"They *will* pull it off," said Nancy, "unless we can stop them. The Marchese's already worked out arrangements to raise the ransom money."

"Which is where your two fake messages come in."

"Check and double check. The messages are designed to accomplish two things: one—to convince the crooks they'll have to work fast before the police raid their hideout, and two—to convince them that if they just let Pietro go, he'll lead them straight to The Prize."

"Okay, Miss Sherlock—sounds like it all adds up," said Don. "At least, you've persuaded *me*. So what happens next?"

"You and I will stake out the Falcone Glassworks tonight and see what happens."

132

# 15

## Stakeout

Twilight was deepening over the lagoon as Nancy and Don made their way across the water to Murano. They were traveling in a small motorboat that belonged to the glassworks. At the Marchese's suggestion, Don had used it to go to Venice, so that he and Nancy could return the same way, without being seen on a public *vaporetto*.

"I still don't understand how you talked the police into letting us handle this on our own," Don remarked.

"I didn't. They don't even know we're coming over here."

Don flashed her a startled glance. "Are you kidding?"

Nancy shook her head. "No, I explained my idea for

tricking the kidnapers into turning Pietro loose, but I didn't offer any guesses as to where he might go. Their strategy, I think, will be to alert every policeman in Venice to be on watch for Pietro throughout the night."

"Why didn't you want them at the glassworks?"

Nancy shrugged. "Maybe I'm wrong, but I had a feeling that once the *carabinieri* got into the act, things might get out of hand. They'd have so many stakeouts and sharpshooters planted all over Murano and around the glass factory, it might give the game away. And if one of them started shooting—well, let's just say I don't *want* any shooting. I think you and I can handle this better on our own."

But was that the whole reason? Nancy wondered, or was it also an excuse to spend some time alone with Don under circumstances that almost *invited* romantic developments? With a nervous pulsebeat, Nancy suddenly realized that she wasn't too sure, even now, if she could answer that question with absolute honesty!

When they reached Murano, Don turned up a canal that eventually brought them to the rear of the glass factory. In the gathering darkness, Nancy saw Zorzi waiting for them on the shallow stone quay. He waved an eager greeting, obviously happy that his vigil was at an end.

"What happened?" Nancy asked him as Don brought the boat alongside and moored it to a cleat.

134

"I give the letter to Signor Rubini like you say. Then I stop in that little *gelateria* across the street from the factory yard and wait, and pretty soon I see him come out and start off toward the boat landing."

"Did you follow him?"

"*Sì*, I keep him in sight all the way, but I make real sure he don't see me!" Zorzi added proudly.

"Good for you!" said Nancy. "So what did he do?"

"He get on the next *vaporetto* and go to Venice."

"Venice!" Don stared in surprise. "But Rubini lives right here on Murano." He paused in silence for a moment, digesting the implications of this. Then he looked at Nancy. "Did you know Rubini was working for the gang?"

"No, but I thought someone at the glassworks might be. There has to be someone at the palazzo who's in their pay, otherwise, who ransacked Tara's and my room? And if they're that thorough about covering all the bases and gleaning all the information they can, then it stands to reason they wouldn't neglect the glassworks, either. After all, this is where Pietro worked."

Don nodded. "Yeah, that figures, I guess."

Nancy paid Zorzi an extra tip besides the five dollars and expense money, and sent him off to catch the next *vaporetto*. Then Don unlocked the loading dock door with his key and they went into the *vetreria*.

Night had fallen. They dared not risk turning on a light, which might be seen from outside. However, several electric lanterns were hanging just inside the loading dock. Don took one and led the way through the one-story building to a closet near the front office where flashlights were kept. Don and Nancy each took one.

"Where would you like to wait?" said Don. He shone the lantern around to refresh Nancy on the plant layout.

"Right here will do—for the time being, at least," said Nancy, gesturing to a small reception area or lobby, furnished with a plastic-covered sofa and end table.

They sat down, side by side, and a thoughtful silence ensued. Enough starlight seeped in through the factory's grimy windows to discern their immediate surroundings.

"Say your plan works," mused Don, "and the crooks let Pietro go. What makes you so sure he'll come here?"

"I'm *not* sure. But I think it's the likeliest possibility."

"Why?"

"Put yourself in Pietro's place. If the gang does intend to trail him, they'll probably try to make him think he escaped by pure luck—you know, by having a guard pretend to fall asleep, or leaving

136

a door 'accidentally' unlocked, something like that."

Don nodded. "So?"

"Eventually he'll want to go to the police or the Marchese, I suppose, and let it be known that he's escaped from his kidnapers. But before that, first of all, if I'm thinking the way Pietro will be thinking, he'll want to make sure The Prize is safe."

"The *Prize?!*" Don was visibly startled, even in the shadowy gloom. "Are you saying it's somewhere here in the glassworks?"

Nancy smiled. "I'm quite sure it is."

"Care to enlarge on that?"

"Not for the moment."

There was another silence. Then Don cleared his throat awkwardly. "Last night at the masquerade ball, you . . . you tried to explain something to me . . ."

"I'd still like to, if you'll listen."

"You don't have to," said Don.

"Maybe not, but please let me."

"Go ahead. I'm listening."

"Gianni switched costumes with you. When I saw him coming in from the terrace, I thought it *was* you. Otherwise I wouldn't have even danced with him. It was only when I noticed the difference in height and when he kissed me that I realized my mistake. And

137

then I didn't want to make a scene—even when he grabbed me and kissed me again. But I was furious, Don. Gianni's really a nasty, twisted character! I told him to leave, or I'd call the servants and have him thrown out as a gate-crasher! That's all, Don. Now do you understand?"

"Of course I understand, Nancy. I acted like a total idiot. There was nothing to get upset about in the first place, if I . . . if I didn't care about you so much. . . . *That's the whole problem!*"

Nancy knit her brows, perplexed. "I don't understand, Don. I'm glad you care about me. I care about you, too. That's why I was so anxious for you to listen."

Don put his head in his hands for a moment. "I'm the one who should explain, Nancy. Do you remember me saying last night that I had other things on my mind?"

"Yes."

"Well, it's true. The main thing on my mind is that I . . . I'm engaged to a girl back home! So what am I doing falling in love with you?!"

The words came tumbling out, as if a dam had suddenly broken. Once having started, Don went on talking, pouring out his heart. "I think I fell for you the first moment I saw you getting off the boat, Nancy, even before we exchanged a word. You bowled me over completely! If I acted gruff and uptight, well, now you know why. I couldn't handle it, not when I already have a fiancee back in Ohio! Coral and I met in college, and we've been going steady ever since. It was love at first sight that time, too, for both of us. Only now I've started dreaming about *you!*"

Nancy listened in a swirl of conflicting emotions— some pleasant, some not so pleasant. Her heart sang when Don said he loved her. She wanted to respond that she loved him, too. But he was somebody else's guy, not hers. He belonged to a girl named Coral, back in Ohio, who expected to marry him . . . and where did that leave a girl from River Heights, named Nancy Drew?

She wasn't quite sure when or how it happened, but suddenly she became aware that she and Don were holding hands in the darkness, and she was telling him all about Ned Nickerson.

"I'm glad you told me, Nancy," Don was saying. "Now I don't feel like such a two-timing, two-faced heel. The same thing happens to lots of people, I suppose . . . even to you, in a way. . . . The only thing is, what are we going to do about it, Nancy?"

He had an arm around her now, and her head was on his shoulder.

"We don't have to make a crisis out of it," she responded softly. "And there's nothing to feel guilty about, either—not if we're honest with ourselves, and . . . and with each other." Nancy reached up and touched his cheek. "There's lots of time to decide. Sooner or later our feelings will sort themselves out, and when they do, then we'll know if what we feel is really love, and who's the most important person in our lives!"

Don was holding her tight now, and her arms were around his neck and their lips were meeting in a kiss that was warm and loving and exciting and, oh so tender! It seemed to Nancy that she'd never, ever before felt about anyone the way she felt about Don Madison at that moment—

They broke apart suddenly as a key turned in the lock of the building's front door—!

# 16

## Night of the Omelet

Don sprang to his feet and pulled Nancy up with him. He looked around swiftly for a place to hide. "Back here, love—!"

He was pointing to a space behind the sofa, shielded by a row of chemical drums. They barely had time to duck down in it when the door opened.

A man came in—husky, dark-haired, thirtyish, in a stained, rumpled suit. Enough moonlight came in from the summer night outside to reveal his face— haggard and unshaven, with a week's growth of beard.

*It was Pietro Rinaldi!* His captors had taken the bait! Nancy felt Don squeeze her hand excitedly.

Pietro left the door open while his eyes became accustomed to the inner darkness. He strode toward the closet for a flashlight. Seconds later, he headed swiftly toward the storeroom where the Falcone glassware was on display. He moved with the tense, single-minded air of a man gripped by a terrible urgency.

Don and Nancy rose from their hiding place and tiptoed after him. He flicked a wall switch, and the storeroom suddenly lit up. Then he began groping and searching among the glass paperweights.

Evidently the one he was looking for wasn't there. His searching became more frantic and desperate. He began muttering aloud, and within moments the mutters became loud explosive curses. Don shot a baffled look at Nancy. She responded by putting a finger to her lips.

They backed quickly into the shadows as Pietro suddenly whirled around and rushed back to the office. They saw him snatch up the handset of a desk phone and start to dial. Moments later, someone must have answered at the other end of the line. Pietro cut loose with angry, frustrated outbursts in Italian, uttered at mile-a-minute speed.

"I don't believe this!" Don gasped in Nancy's ear. "He's talking to Domenic, the butler at the palazzo! It sounds as though th—"

He broke off as Nancy's fingers dug into his arm. Pietro had left the front door slightly ajar—and now it was being pushed open wider. Three people were coming in!

Like fleeting shadows, they moved swiftly toward

the doorway of the plant office. One was a woman; one of the two men held a gun.

At the crucial moment, somebody's foot scuffed a piece of glass and sent it tinkling across the floor. Pietro slammed the phone back in its cradle and whirled to face the doorway.

"Don't try anything foolish!" warned the gunman. Neither his accent nor his words were Italian.

By the light from the office, Nancy could see the faces of the three intruders. The other man was Rubini, the Falcone glassworks manager.

The woman was Katrina van Holst!

"You know what we are after, Pietro, so let us not waste time!" she said crisply. "Give it to us, or you will never leave here alive!"

"It's gone!" Pietro snarled back. "Don't ask me where! Some thieving rat snatched it while your thugs were holding me prisoner! Maybe your stooge Rubini took it! Why don't you ask him?!"

As the furious exchange went on, Don Madison suddenly moved forward on tiptoe. The attention of Katrina and her two companions was concentrated totally on the man in the office, and their angry voices covered any sound of footsteps.

Suddenly Don lunged toward the gunman's back! One arm clamped around the man's neck in a choking grip. His other hand grabbed the intruder's wrist.

Instantly a violent struggle erupted! Pietro rushed at Rubini and staggered him with a fist to the mouth.

143

Nancy grabbed Katrina's long blond hair from behind and tugged with both hands till the Dutch woman screamed.

The gunman dropped his weapon as Don twisted his wrist. A moment later Don sent him flying through the air with a martial-arts body throw. He slammed against the wall and landed on the floor in a stunned heap.

Meanwhile, Don had snatched up the gun and taken charge of the situation. "Hold it—everybody! You three—Katrina, Rubini, you there on the floor—line up with your backs to the wall, and keep your hands in plain sight. Pietro, old pal—I think it's time you did some talking."

"May I say something?" said Nancy.

Don threw her a quizzical grin. "Why not? It was your game plan that brought all these characters out of the woodwork and into the open. Go right ahead."

"Is this what you were looking for, Mr. Rinaldi?" she said and plucked the rainbow glass paperweight out of her shoulder bag.

The expression on Pietro's face was the only answer needed. "Do you know what you are holding there?" he replied in a taut voice that was husky with emotion.

"Drop your gun, Madison!" a voice suddenly broke in. "And if you value your life, do not look around!"

Nancy didn't have to. She knew it was Gianni Spinelli. He must have followed Katrina and her two companions, while they in turn were trailing Pietro.

"Is he bluffing, Pietro?" Don gritted.

The master glassblower shook his head. "No—unfortunately. Better do as he says."

Don let the gun fall to the floor.

"Kick it this way, *grullo!*" Gianni ordered. Turning to Nancy, he added, "And you, *cara,* hand me your pretty little glass egg!"

"Okay, if you insist," said Nancy—and threw the paperweight in his face!

Her move caught Gianni completely unprepared. He jerked his head and flung up an arm to block the glass missile.

Don was on him like a tiger, staggering him with a right cross and kicking the gun out of his hand in a single lightning one-two combination!

The rainbow paperweight lay on the floor, cracked in two. Something was protruding from one of the broken pieces.

Much later that night, Nancy, Don, and Pietro faced Carson Drew, Tara Egan and the Marchese del Falcone in the drawing room of the palace.

Pietro had just finished telling his story. Five years ago in Morocco, he and Rolf Egan had been approached by an I.D.B., or illegal diamond buyer, named Hans Aacht. Over drinks in a Moorish cafe, he described how the world's diamond business was tightly controlled by a single cartel, whose tough security force kept watch over all diamond mining on

145

the African continent. But Aacht was sure he could build up a steady trade in precious stones from native prospectors—if Rolf and Pietro would grubstake him with a few thousand dollars.

For a long time, the scheme yielded little profit. Then one day Aacht showed up in Venice with a huge raw diamond worth half a million dollars. His scheme had finally paid off with a tremendous jackpot!

Unfortunately he had also run afoul of a deadly gang called the *Diamante* Network, which had close ties with the Mafia and considered international diamond smuggling its private domain. They wanted Aacht's life or his huge gemstone.

Aacht had slipped the diamond to Rolf, who in turn passed it to Pietro. Rolf disappeared into a Venetian canal. Pietro also disappeared, supposedly into the hands of professional kidnapers, but actually into the clutches of the Diamante Network, bossed by a beautiful but ruthless woman named Katrina van Holst.

"What about the police?" Tara asked Pietro. "Won't *they* be after you and Hans Aacht for taking the diamond out of Africa?"

Pietro shook his head. "No, because we've committed no crime. It's only the diamond cartel and their security force who try to stop outsiders from trading with native prospectors, as Hans did."

He explained that Hans had feared the Diamante gang might seize Tara and use her as a hostage to force Pietro into surrendering the diamond. But Nancy's clever scheme had forced their hand and tricked them into revealing themselves.

They had, at first, hired Gianni as a spy to help them find Rolf, but out of greed he had tried to grab the diamond for himself.

The apron clue, which Gianni had passed on to the gang, had aroused Katrina's interest in the Faberge egg, so she had helped her gangster gunhand enter the palace disguised as a masquerade party guest. He was the one who had turned out the lights and filched the egg, which, much to her disgust, had proved to contain only counterfeit gems.

"An amazing feat of detection, my dear Nancy!" beamed Francesco del Falcone.

"Now, if only you could find some trace of my father!" Tara added wistfully.

"You've already done that yourself, Tara," Nancy responded lightly.

"Done what?"

"Found a trace of your father. Don't you recall those wet footprints you noticed on our bedroom carpet?"

Tara's eyes became huge. "Oh, Nancy! You're not really implying they could've been made by Daddy's ghost?"

"Why not pinch him and find out?"

"*Pinch* him?!" Tara stared in puzzlement at the teenage sleuth.

"Sure," said Nancy. "There's a cellar dungeon where the Marchese's ancestor hid out that has very wet floors, so the tracks could even have been made by a real flesh-and-blood human. In fact, here comes one right now you might try pinching!"

A tall, bearded blond man had just walked into the room. Tara sprang up with a glad cry, and the two hugged each other so tightly that it seemed as though they were trying to make sure they would never be parted again.

"I tried to let you know I was alive, dear," Rolf Egan told his daughter, "first by slipping that shell into Nancy's suitcase, and then by playing ghost."

"I—I don't understand," said Tara in happy bewilderment. "You mean you've been hiding out here at the palazzo all the time?"

"Yes—ever since I disappeared. Pietro knew about the palace dungeon, so he sneaked me in there one night with Domenic's help. Domenic's known him all his life, you see. We figured I could hide out there till the Diamante gang got off our backs."

Rolf Egan went on to explain that the first time he tried to see Tara at night, she had screamed before he had a chance to take off his false face, leaving him no choice but to flee. The second time he played ghost, he had tried to calm her by whispering her name, but the effect on Tara was still so terrifying that she again screamed in fear.

The ghostly legend of the Marchese's ancestor had

first given Nancy the idea that there might be a secret hiding place at the palazzo. The shell and the ghost calling Tara by name had, together, strengthened Nancy's hunch that Rolf Egan might still be alive and hiding out in the palace.

When he and Tara finally let go of each other, Rolf Egan walked over to clasp Nancy Drew's hand gratefully. She showed him the broken paperweight. A huge raw diamond was sticking out of one of the halves.

"It's a shame such a beautiful work of art has to be ruined just to extract the gemstone. But as somebody once remarked, *To make an omelet, you have to break an egg!*"

# NANCY DREW® MYSTERY STORIES By Carolyn Keene

# THE HARDY BOYS® SERIES By Franklin W. Dixon

- ☐ NIGHT OF THE WEREWOLF—#59
  70993   $3.50
- ☐ MYSTERY OF THE SAMURAI SWORD—#60
  67302   $3.50
- ☐ THE PENTAGON SPY—#61
  67221   $3.50
- ☐ THE APEMAN'S SECRET—#62
  69068   $3.50
- ☐ THE MUMMY CASE—#63
  64289   $3.50
- ☐ MYSTERY OF SMUGGLERS COVE—#64
  66229   $3.50
- ☐ THE STONE IDOL—#65
  69402   $3.50
- ☐ THE VANISHING THIEVES—#66
  63890   $3.50
- ☐ THE OUTLAW'S SILVER—#67
  64285   $3.50
- ☐ DEADLY CHASE—#68
  62477   $3.50
- ☐ THE FOUR-HEADED DRAGON—#69
  65797   $3.50
- ☐ THE INFINITY CLUE—#70
  69154   $3.50
- ☐ TRACK OF THE ZOMBIE—#71
  62623   $3.50
- ☐ THE VOODOO PLOT—#72
  64287   $3.50
- ☐ THE BILLION DOLLAR RANSOM—#73
  66228   $3.50
- ☐ TIC-TAC-TERROR—#74
  66858   $3.50
- ☐ TRAPPED AT SEA—#75
  64290   $3.50
- ☐ GAME PLAN FOR DISASTER—#76
  72321   $3.50
- ☐ THE CRIMSON FLAME—#77
  64286   $3.50
- ☐ CAVE IN—#78
  69486   $3.50
- ☐ SKY SABOTAGE—#79
  62625   $3.50
- ☐ THE ROARING RIVER MYSTERY—#80
  73004   $3.50
- ☐ THE DEMON'S DEN—#81
  62622   $3.50
- ☐ THE BLACKWING PUZZLE—#82
  70472   $3.50

- ☐ THE SWAMP MONSTER—#83
  49727   $3.50
- ☐ REVENGE OF THE DESERT PHANTOM—#84
  49729   $3.50
- ☐ SKYFIRE PUZZLE—#85
  67458   $3.50
- ☐ THE MYSTERY OF THE SILVER STAR—#86
  64374   $3.50
- ☐ PROGRAM FOR DESTRUCTION—#87
  64895   $3.50
- ☐ TRICKY BUSINESS—#88
  64973   $3.50
- ☐ THE SKY BLUE FRAME—#89
  64974   $3.50
- ☐ DANGER ON THE DIAMOND—#90
  63425   $3.50
- ☐ SHIELD OF FEAR—#91
  66308   $3.50
- ☐ THE SHADOW KILLERS—#92
  66309   $3.50
- ☐ THE BILLION DOLLAR RANSOM—#93
  66228   $3.50
- ☐ BREAKDOWN IN AXEBLADE—#94
  66311   $3.50
- ☐ DANGER ON THE AIR—#95
  66305   $3.50
- ☐ WIPEOUT—#96
  66306   $3.50
- ☐ CAST OF CRIMINALS—#97
  66307   $3.50
- ☐ SPARK OF SUSPICION—#98
  66304   $3.50
- ☐ DUNGEON OF DOOM—#99
  69449   $3.50
- ☐ THE SECRET OF ISLAND TREASURE—#100
  69450   $3.50
- ☐ THE MONEY HUNT—#101
  69451   $3.50
- ☐ TERMINAL SHOCK—#102
  69288   $3.50
- ☐ THE MILLION-DOLLAR NIGHTMARE—#103
  69272   $3.50
- ☐ TRICKS OF THE TRADE—#104
  69273   $3.50
- ☐ THE SMOKE SCREEN MYSTERY—#105
  69274   $3.50
- ☐ ATTACK OF THE VIDEO VILLIANS—#106
  69275   $3.50
- ☐ THE HARDY BOYS® GHOST STORIES
  69133   $3.50

**Simon & Schuster, Mail Order Dept. HB5**
**200 Old Tappan Road, Old Tappan, NJ 07675**
Please send me copies of the books checked. Please add appropriate local sales tax.

☐ Enclosed full amount per copy with this coupon (Send check or money order only.)

☐ If order is for $10.00 or more, you may charge to one of the following accounts:

Please be sure to include proper postage and handling:
95¢—first copy
50¢—each additonal copy ordered.

☐ Mastercard   ☐ Visa

Name _____  Credit Card No. _____

Address _____

City _____  Card Expiration Date _____

State _____  Zip _____  Signature _____

Books listed are also available at your local bookstore. Prices are subject to change without notice.   HBD-36